CAIN & ABEL:

A WAR BETWEEN BROTHERS

LaQuanda Washington

July 2025

Copyright Notice

Published by: Kingdom Haven Publishing, LLC
Email: *kingdomhavenpublishingllc@gmail.com*
ISBN: 978-0-9988913-6-1

Then the LORD said to Cain,

"Where is your brother Abel?" "I

don't know," he replied. "Am I

my brother's keeper?"

Genesis 4:9

This book is dedicated to the memory

of:

William Herman Royster

&

Bobby Donnell Matthews, Sr.

You will always be my inspiration!

Love and miss you both, forever!

CHAPTER ONE

As Eva Jamison watched her husband, Adam, sitting cross-legged on the living room floor, playing *Operation* with his twin niece and nephew, a hollow ache settled in her chest. His laughter echoed through the house, full of life and warmth, but all she could feel was the weight of failure pressing down on her. They had been trying to conceive for more than half their marriage. Adam longed to be a father, and Eva had dreamed of being a mother for as long as she could remember. But her doctor's words haunted her: the fibroids complicating her uterus might make it impossible for her to carry a child.

From across the room, Angie—Adam's sister and Eva's closest friend—noticed the sadness clouding Eva's expression. The family had long known about the couple's struggle with infertility, but no one understood Eva's pain better than Angie. She quietly walked over and gently nudged Eva's shoulder.

"Hey, Sis," she said softly, her voice filled with concern. "What's going on?"

Eva swallowed hard against the lump in her throat and blinked back tears. "Hey, Ang," she replied, her voice barely above a whisper, thick with unspoken grief.

"Come on," Angie said, slipping her arm through Eva's. "Let's get some air."

They stepped out onto the deck, then down into the yard where the twilight air was cooler, quieter. Angie wrapped her arms around Eva, holding her in the kind of embrace only twenty years of friendship could offer.

"Eva, I know it's easy for me to say, but you've got to trust God."

"I'm trying, Angie," Eva whispered, tears finally spilling down her cheeks. "I really am. But it's hard. I see him with MJ. and Michelle, and my heart just breaks. I might never be able to give him that."

"Stop talking like that," Angie said firmly, but gently. "We have to stand on God's promises. I don't care what the doctor says, and I don't care what the tests show. The God we serve is a God of miracles—He makes the impossible possible."

Eva wiped her tears and managed a fragile smile. She leaned into her friend's hug, finding comfort in her unwavering faith.

"I knew there was a reason you're my best friend," she whispered.

Angie chuckled. "Trust His timing, Eva. I love the twins with all my heart, but if I'd known I'd be divorced and raising them on my own two years after marrying the man I loved since I was twelve, I might have waited."

Eva winced with empathy. "It's hard enough raising one child with a partner—two on your own? I'm so sorry, Angie."

"Don't apologize," Angie said quickly. "Your pain is real, too. Just believe in God's promise. When the time is right, He'll give you everything you've hoped for—and more."

As they turned back toward the house, the sound of laughter drew their eyes to the yard, where Adam was being gleefully tackled by MJ.

Eva smiled through the remnants of her tears and slipped her arm around Angie's. "What in the world are we going to do with those three?" she asked with a chuckle, watching Adam dramatically fall to the grass.

"Pray for strength," Angie replied, laughing, "and maybe invest in some knee pads."

CHAPTER TWO

Eva couldn't believe what she was hearing. "Are you sure?" She asked the young doctor once more. Dr. Natalie Brown, her gynecologist for the past five years, was giddy with joy. "Yes, I'm sure, Eva," she smiled. She laughed as she patted Eva's hand. "I checked the bloodwork twice, and you are pregnant."

"Lord, thank you!" Eva sobbed as she stared at the computer screen. "There's more", the doctor added softly, "Your ultrasonography and hCG levels indicate that you are expecting twins." Dr. Brown paused a moment to allow Eva to process the shock. Eva inquired softly, "Twins?"

"Yes," Dr. Brown confirmed, struggling to hold back tears of her own.

Natalie had grown close to Eva and Adam over the years, supporting them through multiple miscarriages and false positive pregnancies. Every time she had to break the dreadful news to them, it crushed her heart. She could not contain the excitement she felt. "You're about 16 weeks pregnant. Your tentative due date is September 10th." Eva couldn't help but cry and thank God. "Congratulations, Mommy! Natalie cried."

"I didn't have any signs or symptoms." I didn't think much of my weight gain because my weight has always fluctuated. "Are you certain they're fine?" "Eva, every pregnancy is different," Natalie grinned. Look at your babies, they are perfect" Dr. Brown said, reassuring Eva with the sonogram pictures.

Eva walked out of the doctor's office dazed. She sat in the beautiful lobby of the medical office, watching as a group of pregnant ladies walked by, gripping their tummies. Eva smiled as the women, swollen in various stages of pregnancy, discussed the joys and difficulties of their pregnancies.

While holding the little bag containing her prenatal vitamins, sonogram pictures and pregnancy pamphlets, Eva nervously dialed Adam's number. She couldn't keep her hands from shaking because she was so anxious. She would never be able to drive herself home.

Adam answered the phone on the first ring. "Hey Baby!" Adam smiled, "How are you?" He asked. "I'm good baby, but can you meet me at home?" "Baby, are you okay?" "Yes, I'm fine, I just need to talk to you." "I'm on my way," Adam said, grabbing his briefcase and rushing out of the office.

After conversing with Adam, Eva called Angie. Angie answered the phone on the second ring, "Hey girl," Angie said. "What's up?" "Could you please pick me up from Dr. Brown's office, Angie?" "Um, sure," Angie answered as she shut down her laptop. "I'm leaving right now." Angie dashed out of the house, hoping that Eva was doing well. Eva always told her about her appointments with Dr. Brown. Angie prayed and she rushed to the doctor's office. She didn't think Eva could handle another disappointment.

Adam was anxious; he had never heard Eva sound so frightened. Adam prayed throughout the entire ride home. He had no idea what was wrong, which made him even more terrified. Adam inhaled deeply as he came to a complete stop as the light turned yellow, resisting the urge to speed through the light and hurry home to his wife. "Lord please calm my fears. Help me to believe in you and trust that no matter what happens, you will see us through." Adam immediately felt better. That short prayer immediately calmed his fears. Adam grinned as he reflected on their fifteen-year relationship. Things did not go as planned for either of them, but they were happy. He'd loved Eva from the moment they met. He laughed as he remembered their school days. Urkel and Laura were their nicknames. Eva was Miss Popularity. She was the student body president and the school's cheer captain. Adam never thought he would end up with her in a million years, but here they are more than a decade later and even more in love than they were back then. He knew that no

matter what was going on, together they could conquer the

world.

CHAPTER THREE

Thank You, Lord, Eva whispered silently, tears streaming down her face as she sat motionless in the small waiting area, her trembling hands resting protectively over her abdomen. Her heart raced, still trying to catch up with the news she'd just received. After years of failed tests, invasive procedures, and tearful prayers whispered in the dark, the impossible had happened—she was pregnant.

She had stopped asking. She had stopped hoping. Somewhere along the way, Eva had gently laid her dream of motherhood on the altar and decided to embrace whatever future God had planned for her and Adam, even if that meant adoption. She had made peace with it. Or so she thought.

But now?

"I can't believe I'm pregnant," she whispered again, her voice catching in her throat as her hand gently caressed the

curve of her belly, still flat but now sacred. "Oh, God...
You remembered me."

Just then, the sound of quick footsteps echoed in the
hallway. Angie burst into the lobby, scanning the room
until her eyes found Eva seated near the window, her face a
portrait of awe and disbelief. Angie's voice was soft,
almost reverent, when she finally spoke. "Hi, Evie."

The moment Eva heard her best friend's voice, whatever
composure she had managed to cling to shatter completely.
She shot up from her seat and rushed into Angie's arms
with such force that Angie nearly stumbled backward.

For a long time, they just stood there, holding each other in
a wordless embrace. It was the kind of hug that held years
of shared prayers, silent cries, and late-night conversations
filled with faith and fear alike. When Eva finally pulled
back, her face was streaked with tears and glowing with
joy.

"I'm pregnant, Angie," she breathed, her voice breaking under the weight of the words. "I'm really pregnant."

Angie's eyes widened in astonishment before filling with tears of her own. "Oh my God," she gasped, pressing both hands to her mouth. "Eva, are you serious?"

"Yes!" Eva sobbed, laughing and crying all at once. "I had the bloodwork done. It's real. I even saw the little heartbeat on the monitor."

Angie let out a cry of joy as the two women held each other again, swaying slightly in the middle of the clinic lobby. Onlookers turned to watch—some offering polite smiles, others clearly puzzled by the emotional scene. A few, however, recognized that kind of joy. Women who had walked similar roads of longing paused to wipe their eyes or quietly offered congratulations, as though they, too, had received a victory that day.

Later, as they sat in Angie's car in the parking lot, the atmosphere between them was reverent, like sacred ground had been walked on.

"Angie," Eva said quietly, almost as if speaking too loudly would wake her from a dream. "I still can't believe it. After everything... I really thought maybe God had a different plan for us. I gave up, Ang. I stopped asking. I didn't think I could take another 'no.' I feel almost ashamed admitting it."

"But look at God," Angie said, her voice thick with emotion, eyes shimmering with tears. "Girl, I don't care how long it took—He still came through. Right on time. That baby in your belly is living proof that His promises never come back void."

Eva leaned back in her seat, resting her hand on her stomach again. "You know what's crazy? I thought I'd be shouting and dancing when this day came. But all I feel right now is this deep, quiet peace. Like something in me has finally come full circle."

Angie smiled and reached for Eva's hand. "That's the peace that comes when you've surrendered your plans to God and then watch Him give you back more than you ever thought possible. He's faithful, Sis. Always."

A silence fell between them, not awkward, but warm— holy. The kind of silence that only two best friends of twenty years can share, when words aren't needed because the heart already understands.

Eva turned her gaze out the window, watching the world move by outside—cars coming and going, people laughing, living. Everything seemed different now. Brighter. More alive.

She closed her eyes, took a deep breath, and whispered one more time, "Thank You, Lord."

CHAPTER FOUR

The car had barely rolled to a stop before Adam flung open the door and sprinted toward the house. The urgency in Eva's voice during their brief call had shaken him, and he couldn't get home fast enough.

"Baby? Where are you?" he called as he burst through the front door, his keys still dangling from the lock.

"I... I'm in the bedroom," Eva called out, her voice soft, trembling with a mix of nerves and excitement. Her heart thudded wildly against her ribcage, as if it already knew this moment would change everything.

Adam bounced up the stairs and into their bedroom, breathless. The worry on his face dissolved the moment he saw her sitting on the edge of the bed, her eyes shimmering.

"Eva, are you okay?" he asked, rushing to her side and dropping to his knees, his hands gently cradling hers.

"Yes, baby. I'm fine—actually..." she paused, giggling through a tearful smile, "...I'm more than fine."

Adam blinked at her, still concerned. "You sounded... I don't know, different on the phone. I was scared something happened."

Eva's eyes locked onto his. "We're okay, baby. *We're just fine.*"

He exhaled, visibly relieved, running a hand over his face. "Thank God. You had me thinking—" He stopped short. Something in her eyes—something glowing and unspoken—caught him off guard. "Wait... what do you mean *we*?"

She smiled, the joy on her face radiating like morning sun. Her voice was barely a whisper. "Adam… we're pregnant."

Adam's eyes widened. He blinked, stunned, the words echoing in his ears before sinking in. "We're—" His hands instinctively reached for her belly, and he kissed it with reverence.

"Baby... are you serious?" His voice cracked, choked by rising emotion.

"I'm sure," Eva said, tears slipping down her cheeks. She reached for the small envelope on the nightstand and gently placed it in his hands. "Look."

Adam stared at the black-and-white sonogram images with trembling fingers, his breath catching as he traced the outlines. "Oh my God… this is real. This is really happening."

Eva brushed her thumb across his cheek, her own voice thick with tears. "Those are our babies."

He looked up sharply. "Wait—*babies*?"

She nodded, laughing through happy sobs. "Yes, Adam. Twins."

Adam shot to his feet, momentarily forgetting how to use his legs. He stumbled backward, his face a perfect mixture of shock and overwhelming joy.

"Sit down before you pass out, Daddy," Eva teased, patting the bed.

He obeyed, collapsing beside her, laughing and crying all at once. He buried his face into the crook of her neck, wrapping his arms tightly around her as he whispered over and over again, "Thank You, Jesus. Thank You. Thank You."

They stayed like that for a long time, wrapped in each other's arms, their tears soaking into the sheets as they whispered prayers of gratitude. It felt like heaven had bent low and touched their home, answering years of longing in a single divine moment.

Later, still curled up in bed, Adam lay beside Eva, one hand protectively resting on her belly. His eyes never strayed far from the sonogram photos resting on the nightstand.

"I've never seen you this happy," Eva murmured, her voice filled with wonder.

"That's because I've never *been* this happy," Adam replied, brushing a strand of hair from her forehead. "I'd dreamt about this day, but nothing could've prepared me for how it actually feels."

Eva smiled, but her fingers unconsciously returned to her belly, gently circling over the place where their babies were growing. Joy was there, yes—but so was fear.

She closed her eyes and whispered, barely audible, "Lord, please… let me carry them to term. Let them live."

Adam must've sensed her shift, because he turned to her and gently cupped her cheek. "We're going to be okay," he said softly. "*They're* going to be okay. This isn't just something we prayed for—this is something God promised."

Eva nodded, but the uncertainty still lingered in her eyes. They had been here before—excitement, hope, loss. The memory of past heartbreak hadn't disappeared. It clung quietly to the edges of her joy.

But tonight, as Adam held her, and she held the promise growing inside of her, she allowed herself to hope again. To believe again.

For the first time in a long time, she wasn't afraid to dream.

CHAPTER FIVE

The next five months flew by in a blur of doctor appointments, baby showers, nursery preparations, and midnight cravings. Eva and Adam had spent nearly every moment soaking in the joy—and the surreal reality—that they were finally going to be parents to twin boys.

Now, the day had arrived.

Eva lay propped up in the hospital bed, her Bible open across her lap. The words of Psalm 127 had comforted her all morning: *"Children are a heritage from the Lord, the fruit of the womb a reward."* She read it again, whispering it like a prayer.

Across the room, Adam was in full-on dad mode, pacing back and forth as he checked—and rechecked—the hospital bag for what had to be the third or fourth time in the last hour. He moved with focused intensity, as if he were preparing for a military operation.

Eva watched him with quiet amusement, a soft smile playing on her lips.

"Sweetheart," she finally said, her voice warm but teasing, "I think it's safe to say we've packed everything short of the kitchen sink."

Adam looked up, sheepishly grinning. "I know. I just want to make sure we have everything the boys and you might need. Diapers, blankets, onesies, snacks, chargers—"

"Baby," she interrupted gently, "you've been amazing. Truly. I don't know how I would've gotten through these past few months without you."

He crossed the room and sat beside her, his hand finding hers as he smiled. "Oh, you mean you weren't your usual sunshine-and-rainbows self?" he joked, dodging a playful slap on the arm.

"I'm serious," Eva said, squeezing his hand. "I know I haven't exactly been easy lately. Between the mood swings, cravings, back pain—and unsolicited crying at laundry detergent commercials," Adam added with a grin.

Eva laughed, then leaned her head against his shoulder. "Still, you never complained. You've been my rock, Adam."

"Eva," he said softly, cupping her face and looking into her eyes, "you've given me the two most precious gifts in the world. I would walk through fire for you and our boys. Whatever comes next—we're in it together."

Tears welled in Eva's eyes as he leaned in and kissed her gently. She rested her hand on her belly. "We love you too, Daddy."

Adam kissed her forehead and whispered, "I love you all more, Mommy."

Just then, the door swung open, and a familiar voice rang out.

"Well, Mommy and Daddy—it's showtime!" Dr. Natalie Brown stepped into the room with a bright smile and a clipboard in hand.

"Hey, Doc!" Adam stood and pulled her into a quick hug. "Thanks for getting us to the finish line."

"We're almost there," Dr. Brown said cheerfully, then turned to Eva with a warm, reassuring smile. "How are we feeling?"

"Nervous. Excited. A little overwhelmed," Eva admitted honestly, her voice slightly shaky. "But ready... I think."

"As ready as we'll ever be," Adam added, giving her hand another squeeze.

Dr. Brown placed a hand on Eva's shoulder. "There's nothing to be afraid of. God has brought you both this far— and He's going to carry you the rest of the way. Just breathe. Trust Him."

Eva nodded, blinking away tears. "It's the *after* part I keep thinking about," she said quietly. "I've never been a mother before. I don't know what I'm doing."

Dr. Brown smiled gently. "Neither did any of the billions of women who became mothers before you. But somehow, they all figured it out. And so will you."

"She's right," Adam chimed in, leaning over to kiss Eva's cheek. "You're going to be the most incredible mom. Those boys are so lucky."

A nurse entered the room then, gently announcing it was time to be prepped for the surgery. Adam stood and helped Eva swing her legs slowly over the side of the bed.

Dr. Brown paused at the door. "In less than an hour," she said, her voice full of warmth, "you'll be holding two little miracles in your arms."

Eva looked up at Adam, her eyes filled with wonder and gratitude. "We really made it," she whispered.

Adam brushed a tear from her cheek. "No, baby… God

brought us here."

With that, they wheeled her toward the operating room,

hearts pounding with anticipation and awe.

In just moments, their long-awaited promise would become

reality.

CHAPTER SIX

The bright lights of the delivery room shimmered against the soft beeping of monitors, sterile and clinical—yet sacred. For all her anxiety and years of waiting, Eva felt an unexpected calm wash over her. Her fingers tightened around Adam's as the medical team worked methodically, voices low and focused.

Though her labor had been long—nearly sixteen hours from the first contraction to the final push—Dr. Brown had called it a miracle in motion. Considering Eva's complex medical history, including her fibroids and past losses, this delivery had been smoother than anyone had expected. It was long, yes—but mercifully free of complications. God had truly gone before them.

Then it happened.

A tiny, sharp cry pierced the room like music. Eva gasped, her heart exploding with joy and disbelief. Her eyes flooded with tears as she turned toward the sound, her lips trembling.

"That's our son," Adam whispered, awe-struck, his own voice cracking as he leaned in to kiss her forehead. "That's *our* son."

She couldn't speak. Her soul was overwhelmed with a love so fierce it left her breathless.

A few moments later, the room was filled with the cries of another newborn. Twin voices—twin miracles.

Adam's knees nearly buckled. His hands flew to his mouth as he watched the nurses gently cleaned and wrapped the tiny boys in soft, blue blankets. When they handed him both of his sons, the full weight of the moment crashed into his chest.

He wept.

Tears poured down his face as he looked from one perfect little face to the other. Their eyes were shut tight, lips puckered, tiny fists waving in the air as if announcing their arrival.

"They're perfect," he choked out, turning to Eva. "They're absolutely perfect."

Eva nodded weakly from the bed, tears streaming down her cheeks, her chest aching with joy.

"Cain and Abel," Adam whispered reverently, holding them close. The names they had prayed over. The names that carried stories of firstborns and second chances.

"Thank You, Lord," he whispered, barely audible, overcome with emotion.

He turned toward Eva, his smile stretching ear to ear.

"Come on, boys," he said gently, rocking them. "Let's go meet your mommy."

He brought them over, carefully positioning himself so Eva could see them both. The second her eyes met theirs—miniature versions of Adam with the same strong brow, the same heart-shaped lips—her soul gave way to a deeper kind of love she hadn't known was possible.

"They're beautiful," Eva sobbed. "They look just like you," Adam said at the exact same time she did.

They both laughed through their tears, caught in the surreal joy of the moment.

Dr. Brown, now standing beside them with a gentle smile, chuckled. "I'd say they look like a perfect blend of you both," she said, wiping a tear from her cheek. "They are absolute miracles. Every single part of this moment is a testimony."

Eva nodded, barely able to respond. Her eyes closed as she breathed deeply, her heart full, her body exhausted but satisfied. She said nothing out loud, but her soul prayed the loudest prayer she'd ever offered.

Thank You, God. Thank You for bringing us through.

Thank You for remembering me. For remembering us. For these boys—for this family.

Adam leaned down, pressing a kiss on her forehead, then one on each baby's cheek. "You did it, Eva," he whispered. "We did it."

As the medical staff gently cleaned up around them, dimming the lights and giving them privacy, Eva and Adam lay together, side by side, their newborn sons nestled between them. A sacred stillness fell over the room, the kind only heaven could orchestrate.

Cain stirred first, followed by a soft whimper from Abel. Their parents looked at each other, eyes wide and full of joy.

"Looks like they already have a lot to say," Adam whispered, grinning.

Eva smiled, exhausted but radiant. "Just like their daddy." They both laughed softly, then fell silent again—content to simply *be* in the presence of answered prayers.

CHAPTER SEVEN

"Happy Father's Day, Daddy!" Cain and Abel shouted in unison as they burst into their parents' bedroom, their small feet thudding against the hardwood floor before they leapt onto the bed, giggling.

Adam jolted awake with a laugh as two sets of arms wrapped around him. He pulled them close, his heart full.

"Thank you, boys," he said warmly, embracing them tightly. "What a way to wake up!"

"Daddy, I made this for you," Abel said proudly, holding up a colorful hand-drawn card made from construction paper and love. Glitter clung to his fingers, and the handwriting was a little wobbly, but Adam's face lit up as he took the handmade gift.

"Aww, Abel," Adam said, his voice catching slightly. "This is amazing. I love it. Best card ever!"

Before Adam could finish admiring it, Cain shoved his way forward, nearly knocking the card from his father's hand.

"Here, Daddy," Cain said, thrusting a glossy store-bought card into Adam's lap. "I bought this one with my allowance. It's better than that dumb card Abel made."

The room fell uncomfortably quiet for a beat.

Adam sat up straighter, his tone shifting as he looked Cain directly in the eyes. "Hey, Cain," he said firmly, but gently. "We don't tear others down to lift ourselves up—especially not your brother."

Cain looked away, arms folded tightly across his chest.

"Abel worked hard on that card, and I love it because it came from his heart. Just like I love yours—because *you* gave it. But what makes something special isn't how much it costs… it's how much love is in it."

He turned to Abel and ruffled his hair. "Thank you, buddy. I love both cards. They're perfect."

But Cain's face had already soured. His eyes narrowed, jaw clenched. Without a word, he jumped off the bed and stormed out of the room, leaving a trail of tension in his wake.

Adam sighed deeply, his smile faltering.

He loved both his sons with everything in him—but they couldn't have been more different. Abel was cheerful, generous, and quick to forgive. Cain, on the other hand, had always carried something heavy in his heart. Even when they were toddlers, Adam had noticed Cain's deep longing to be first… to be *seen*. His jealousy toward Abel wasn't new—it had been slowly growing, like a thorn working its way deeper over time.

He and Eva had tried everything: one-on-one outings, positive affirmations, even sessions with a child therapist. Still, Cain struggled. And Adam, more than anything, just wanted to understand how to love his son the *way* he needed to be loved.

"God," Adam whispered under his breath, watching the door Cain had disappeared through, "help me reach him.

Help me love him the way You love us. Fully. Patiently. Unconditionally."

Meanwhile, Eva, who had been listening from the hallway, quietly followed their older son into the twins' bedroom. She found Cain curled on the floor in the corner, his arms wrapped around his knees, fighting back tears. She didn't say anything at first. She simply sat down beside him.

After a few moments, she placed a gentle hand on his back. "Sweetheart… what's going on?"

Cain sniffled, trying to keep his voice from trembling.

"Everybody loves Abel," he said finally, his words small and jagged. "Nobody loves me."

Eva's heart broke at the rawness in his voice.

"Oh, Cain… that couldn't be further from the truth," she said softly. "Your daddy and I love you both so much. You and Abel are different, yes—but that just means you both bring something special into our family."

Cain looked down at the floor. "You always say Abel's good. Everyone always likes him better."

Eva turned to face him completely, gently lifting his chin so he would meet her eyes.

"Let me tell you something," she said, her voice tender but steady. "For many years, your father and I didn't think we would ever be able to have a baby. We prayed and cried and waited a long time. And then one day—God answered. Not with one baby. But with *two*. You and your brother." She smiled, brushing a strand of hair off his forehead. "We rejoiced over you, Cain. You are an answered prayer. We still pray for you every single day."

Cain's lip trembled, and a single tear escaped down his cheek.

"Do you know what your name means?" Eva continued.

Cain shook his head.

"It means 'acquired' or 'possessed,'" she said. "Because when I held you for the first time, I knew you were a gift straight from God's hand. A son He gave to me after I thought I might never be a mother."

Cain couldn't hold it in anymore. He leaned into her and sobbed against her shoulder. Eva wrapped her arms around him and held him tightly, stroking his hair, kissing his forehead.

"I love you, Cain," she whispered. "Nothing you do will ever change that."

As she rocked him gently, her heart cried out again in silent prayer.

Lord, show us how to reach him. Heal whatever wounds we can't see. Help him feel the depth of the love we have for him—the love You have for him. Let him know that he is enough.

CHAPTER EIGHT

"Come on, Abel," Cain called, glancing over his shoulder as he stepped deeper into the woods. "Stop being such a scaredy-cat."

"I'm not scared," Abel replied, hesitating at the edge of the tree line. His voice was firm, but his feet stayed planted. "But Mama said we're not supposed to come over here."

Cain rolled his eyes. "We're not gonna be long. I just want to check out the snake pit by the creek."

Abel grimaced. "Snakes are gross. Let's just go home."

Cain smirked, the corners of his mouth twitching with mischief. "You always ruin everything. Come on—it'll be quick."

Reluctantly, Abel followed, stepping carefully over fallen branches and dry leaves. The deeper they went, the darker it became under the canopy of trees.

"There," Cain said suddenly, pointing to a patch of tall grass. "I think I see one."

He crouched down slowly, pretending to examine the ground. Abel crept closer behind him, squinting to see.

"Where?"

Before he could finish, Cain sprang up and flung something long and black in his direction.

Abel screamed.

It was a snake—small and harmless, but alive and very real.

He turned and bolted out of the woods, his cries echoing through the trees.

Cain burst into laughter. "Abel, come on! It's just a little snake!"

But as he jogged after his brother, the smile vanished from his face. Abel wasn't stopping. He was running blindly— straight toward the road.

"Abel, wait! STOP!" Cain shouted, but his voice caught in his throat as he spotted a silver car barreling down the street.

Time slowed.

Abel never looked up.

The impact came with a sickening thud, the sound echoing in Cain's ears like a thunderclap. Abel's body was thrown into the air before crashing onto the pavement with a lifeless thump.

"ABEL!" Cain screamed, his feet pounding against the ground as he raced to his brother's side. His legs nearly gave out beneath him as he dropped to his knees beside Abel's small, crumpled frame.

Blood stained the pavement. Abel's eyes were shut, his limbs twisted unnaturally. Cain reached out with a trembling hand, gently touching his brother's shoulder. "Please," he whispered. "Please wake up. I didn't mean it…"

His chest tightened, and tears poured down his face. "I'm sorry, Abel… I didn't mean to hurt you."

In the distance, the wail of sirens grew louder. A nearby ambulance that had been stationed for a neighborhood event came screeching around the corner.

Cain was still kneeling beside his brother when the paramedics arrived, quickly pushing him aside as they began administering CPR.

"No—please let me stay!" Cain sobbed, but they were already working.

He rocked back on his heels; arms wrapped tightly around his stomach as he cried out to God. "Please don't let him die. Please, please…"

Then, another voice broke through the chaos—one full of fear and anguish.

"ABEL! CAIN!"

Cain turned just in time to see his mother running down the sidewalk, neighbors trying and failing to hold her back. Her screams cut into his soul.

Eva dropped beside the paramedics, clutching Abel's hand before they could lift him onto the stretcher. "What happened? Cain, what happened?" she cried, her voice trembling.

Cain tried to speak. His mouth opened, but no words came. Only sobs. He collapsed onto the pavement, burying his face in his hands.

It was my fault.

He hadn't meant for this to happen. He'd just wanted to scare Abel—not hurt him. Not this.

Cain watched through watery eyes as Eva climbed into the back of the ambulance with her youngest son. Moments later, strong arms scooped Cain off the pavement.

"Got you, buddy," said a man's voice, low and kind.

Cain couldn't see who it was. Everything was a blur.

Voices shouted around him—someone yelled to call Adam.

The weight of guilt grew heavier by the second.

Then it hit him—his stomach churned violently, and he vomited all over the man's shoes.

"It's okay," the man said gently, rubbing his back. "You're in shock. It's going to be okay."

But Cain knew that wasn't true.

Nothing would ever be okay again—not if Abel died.

His chest ached as he looked up just in time to see the ambulance turning the corner, sirens screaming into the distance. He pressed his hands together, tears soaking his cheeks.

"Please, God," he whispered. "Forgive me. And please… please don't let my brother die."

CHAPTER NINE

It had been eleven long months since the accident—months filled with hospital visits, physical therapy, and countless prayers. And finally, Abel was walking again without the help of crutches.

Cain watched his brother take a few careful steps across the living room. Though Abel still limped slightly, there was a newfound lightness in his movement.

"Hey man," Cain said, trying to sound casual. "How's it feel? Being crutch-free?"

Abel grinned, his smile genuine. "It feels amazing. Like I'm free again."

Cain nodded, but a heaviness tugged at his chest. "Abel... I just—I really am sorry," he said suddenly, his voice cracking. "I never meant for you to get hurt."

Abel turned toward his brother and looked him in the eyes. "I know that, Cain," he said gently. "I know you'd never do anything to hurt me on purpose."

The words offered some relief, but not enough to erase the guilt Cain had been carrying for nearly a year. Abel might have forgiven him—but Cain wasn't sure their parents had. The memory of that day—the accident, the sirens, the look in his mother's eyes when he finally told the truth—was seared into his mind. It wasn't the punishment that had broken him. It was the disappointment etched into their faces. The silent question: *How could you?*

"I don't think Mom and Dad have gotten over it," Cain said, barely above a whisper. "Not really."

"They're not mad anymore, Cain," Abel replied, lowering himself carefully onto the couch. "That was months ago. They were scared, not angry."

Cain shook his head, fists clenched. "It doesn't matter. I always mess things up. No matter what I do, it's never enough."

Abel watched him carefully.

"I've been trying my whole life to make them proud," Cain continued, tears burning in the corners of his eyes. "But they never look at me the way they look at you. You're the miracle baby. The one who survived. The one who always does everything right."

Cain's voice grew bitter. "I wish I could be more like you... but I'm not perfect."

Abel's expression softened. "Cain, neither am I. I make mistakes too. Just because I don't get in trouble as much doesn't mean I don't fall short. I'm not perfect—and no one expects you to be either."

"Tell that to Mom and Dad," Cain muttered, his eyes narrowing.

Abel didn't respond immediately. He had learned over time that when Cain was like this—heavy with emotion, guilt, and frustration—one wrong word could ignite the fire inside him.

Cain stood up suddenly, his body tense. Without a word, he stormed out of the room and slammed the door behind him, the echo of it reverberating down the hallway like thunder.

Abel sat in silence, staring after his brother. He exhaled slowly, trying to calm the unease rising in his chest.

There was something about Cain's anger—an intensity that didn't just flare; it simmered. It made Abel feel like he was standing on a fault line, never knowing when it might crack open beneath him.

Even as children, Abel had sensed that Cain's emotions ran deeper than anyone realized. But lately… that feeling had shifted. It wasn't just sadness or frustration anymore. It was something darker. Something dangerous.

And it terrified him.

He didn't know what to say, or what to do. So, he did the only thing he could think of.

Abel bowed his head, folded his hands, and prayed.

God, please help my brother. Heal whatever is broken

inside him. Give him peace, Lord... before his pain

becomes something he can't control.

CHAPTER TEN

Graduation day had finally arrived—a milestone that marked the end of one chapter and the beginning of another. For the Jamison twins, Cain and Abel, it was a day of excitement, though their reasons couldn't have been more different.

Abel was radiant, his face glowing with pride and anticipation. He had worked tirelessly for this moment, and it had all paid off. Not only had he been accepted into all seven universities he'd applied to, but he had also earned full scholarships to each one. To top it off, he'd been named valedictorian of their senior class.

Cain, on the other hand, could hardly wait for the ceremony to be over. He slouched in the back seat of the car, arms crossed, his eyes locked on the passing scenery outside the window as his parents gushed once again about how proud they were of Abel.

"You've made us so proud, son," Adam said, placing a hand on Abel's shoulder from the front seat. "We always knew you had it in you."

"We're so excited to see where God is going to take you next," Eva added, her eyes misty with emotion.

Cain rolled his eyes and shifted uncomfortably. He knew they meant well, but their words felt like a spotlight exposing every one of his failures.

He didn't hate Abel—at least not completely—but he hated how small he always felt when Abel was around. It was like no matter what he did, he was never good enough. Abel was the golden boy, the miracle child who had come back from the brink of death and grown into everything their parents had ever hoped for. Cain was the reminder that not every child shines the same way.

Where Abel saw education as a gateway to opportunity, Cain saw it as a prison he'd finally escaped. College was never part of his plan. The very thought of more classrooms, more rules, more comparisons made his skin crawl. All he wanted was freedom—a job, his own money, and a space where he didn't feel like he had to compete just to be noticed.

Adam and Eva had tried to push college, gently at first, then more persistently as the year went on. But Cain was stubborn, unyielding as ever. If they said go left, he'd go right—just to remind them he wasn't Abel.

In the end, Adam gave up the fight. He loved his son deeply, but he refused to invest money into something Cain had no heart for. "He has to want it," Adam had told Eva. "I won't force him into a future he'll end up resenting." Still, the disappointment lingered.

Two years later, Cain had finally scraped together enough savings to move into his own apartment. It was small, sparsely furnished, and sat above an aging convenience store—but it was his. No more curfews. No more questions. No more eyes watching his every move.

Cain closed the door behind him with a satisfied thud and leaned against it, soaking in the silence. For the first time, no one was asking where he was going or who he'd be with. He dropped his keys on the counter, kicked off his shoes, and made his way to the secondhand couch Aunt Angie had given him.

He flopped down with a contented sigh and reached into the side drawer, pulling out a pack of cigarettes. Lighting one with a flick of his thumb, he inhaled deeply and exhaled slowly, watching the smoke curl into the air.

He wasn't allowed to smoke at his parents' house—not even outside. But now?

Now he could do what he wanted.

He propped his feet up on the wobbly coffee table, leaned back, and smiled to himself. The apartment might've been modest, but to Cain, it was freedom wrapped in peeling paint and secondhand furniture.

He felt powerful. Independent. In control.

For the first time in his life, Cain felt like he was on top of

the world.

CHAPTER ELEVEN

Cain stared out the window of the bus, the world blurring past like memories he couldn't quite grasp. Five years. So much had changed in that time, and yet, here he was—finally coming home. Determined not to repeat the mistakes of his past, he vowed silently that this would be his last time behind bars. He'd lost so much already—the births of his twin daughters, the last five of his son's seven birthdays. Those moments haunted him, fueling a fierce resolve to make things right.

The bus came to a halt, and Cain stepped down onto the familiar pavement. Abel was waiting with a smile that warmed the chill in Cain's chest.

"Welcome home, bro," Abel said, wrapping him in a tight hug.

"Thanks, man," Cain replied, returning the smile, though his eyes still carried the weight of the years.

Abel stepped back, studying him. "Wow, you've really grown. I almost didn't recognize you."

"Yeah," Cain said with a half-smile. "Had to keep busy, keep my mind off the time."

"Well, it's good to have you back," Abel said, clapping him on the shoulder. "Come on—Ma and Dad are waiting at the house."

They walked to a sleek black Mercedes with paper tags still taped to the window. Cain inhaled deeply as he slid into the leather seat, the new car scent sharp and clean.

"This is nice," Cain said, running his hand over the soft leather.

Abel grinned. "Thanks. I treated myself when I graduated from law school."

Cain nodded, impressed. "Congrats, little brother. Never thought I'd see you studying to be a judge."

Abel laughed. "Me neither. But I fell in love with the law."

"Well, I'm proud of you. We need more men like you on the bench."

"That we do," Abel agreed.

There was a brief pause before Abel asked, "So enough about me. What about you? What's next?"

Cain rolled his eyes. "Man, I just got home. Can I have one day without you grilling me?"

Abel smirked. "My bad. Didn't mean to pressure you. Nobody expects you to have it all figured out right away."

"Yeah, right," Cain muttered, frustration creeping back. "Tell that to Ma and Dad. Every time I call, the first question is always 'What are your plans when you come home?'"

"They're just glad you're back. And Cam and the kids—they're waiting for you too."

Cain's eyes flickered, and he rolled them again. Cam—his wife, his high school sweetheart. The love of his life and mother to their three children. He loved them fiercely. But his struggle to provide the life he dreamed of had landed him in jail twice in five years. And the thought of those twin daughters, babies he'd never held in his arms—that cut deeper than anything else.

"I gotta do better," Cain whispered, more to himself than anyone else.

Abel glanced at his brother, the weight of Cain's unspoken pain clear in his eyes. Quietly, he prayed—for strength, for healing, and that this time, Cain's road home would be final.

CHAPTER TWELVE

Cain sat on the worn couch, rubbing his temples as exhaustion and frustration gnawed at him. It had been two weeks since he'd come home, and he was trying—really trying—to be the father his twin daughters, Hailey and Bailey, needed. But those years behind bars, starting when Cam was eight months pregnant, had created a chasm between them. Now almost six, the girls barely knew him. Their cautious eyes and hesitant steps whenever he approached made the distance painfully clear.

His son, CJ, was nearly eight and already taller than Cam, a quiet testament to all the milestones Cain had missed. Every moment of their lives had unfolded without him, and the absence weighed heavily on his heart. They shied away from him, retreating into the comfort of anyone but him— including their Uncle Abel, who seemed to have slipped effortlessly into the role Cain longed to reclaim.

"It's going to take time, Cain," Cam said softly, settling beside him on the couch. Her hand found his, offering quiet support.

Cain sighed, the weight of his own impatience pressing down. "I know," he admitted, "but it doesn't make it any easier when they keep calling me 'Abel.'

Cam gave a gentle, understanding smile. "I know it's hard. But for years, it's just been the four of us. They're still adjusting to having another person in their lives. They will come around—you just have to give them space and time."

Cain's jaw tightened. "I'm not just 'another person,' Cam. I'm their father."

She squeezed his hand reassuringly. "I know, love. But remember—you were the one who asked me not to bring them to visit you while you were gone. Seeing pictures of their dad is one thing. Having you here in person is something completely different. They know you're their dad, but they're still getting used to the idea of you being part of their everyday lives."

Cain leaned back, closing his eyes and taking a deep breath, trying to steady the turmoil inside him. "I understand," he said quietly. Then, almost without thinking, he stood abruptly. "I'll come back tomorrow." Without another word, he left the room.

Cam wiped the tears that had quietly slipped down her cheeks. She had loved Cain since their freshman year of high school—loved him fiercely and without hesitation. But the anger inside him had grown heavier with each passing year, spreading like a shadow over everything. When they were young, her youthful hope had convinced her that love alone could heal him, that it could drive away the pain that haunted him. But now she knew better. Those demons were Cain's to fight. No matter how much she loved him, she couldn't battle his darkness for him.

With a quiet prayer whispered into the stillness, Cam rose

to prepare dinner for the kids, holding on to hope that

someday, maybe soon, Cain would find his way back—not

just to them, but to himself.

CHAPTER THIRTEEN

Cain ripped the letter into pieces, each tear fueled by frustration and defeat. He threw the shreds across the room, watching them flutter like fallen leaves.

"Hey, big bro, what's going on?" Abel asked quietly, stepping into the room and surveying the scattered paper.

Cain sank onto the couch, rubbing his face tiredly. "That's the third rejection letter this week. Third one. I don't know what else to do, Abel. All I want is a job—a way to provide for my family." His voice cracked slightly, betraying the weight he carried.

Abel pulled up a chair and sat beside him, placing a steady hand on Cain's shoulder. "I know, Cain. Something will come along. It has to."

"Yeah, well, that's easier to say than believe right now," Cain muttered.

Abel hesitated for a moment, then reached into his pocket. "Actually, that's part of the reason I came over. I've been saving some money for a while. I want you to have it. I figured things might be tight, and this could help you get back on your feet."

Cain looked up, eyes narrowing. "Abel, I really appreciate that. But I can't take it."

"Why not?" Abel asked, genuinely curious.

"Because I'm a man, Abel. I have to take care of my own family. I can't have another man doing it for me. Besides," Cain's voice grew softer, "my kids already call you 'Abel' more than they call me 'Dad.'"

Abel's grip on Cain's shoulder tightened just a little. "Cain, this is just between us. No one else has to know. And if the situation were reversed, you'd do the exact same thing for me without hesitation."

Cain sighed, a mix of pride and stubbornness swirling inside him. "I know you mean well, and I truly appreciate it. But those kids. They're mine. I'm going to find a way to provide for them myself. I'm home now, and it's my responsibility. Thanks for looking out for them when I couldn't, but it's time I stepped up, okay?"

Abel smiled sadly, knowing there was no changing Cain's mind when he got like this. "Sure, Cain. I get it." He stood and clapped his brother on the back. "How about this? Let's go grab a bite to eat. My treat."

Cain shook his head, a small smile breaking through his frustration. "Alright, but only because I'm starving."

Abel laughed, glad to see even the smallest light in Cain's eyes. "Deal. And maybe one day soon, you'll let me help without the fight."

Cain smiled, grateful for the bond that kept them connected, no matter how hard the road got.

CHAPTER FOURTEEN

Cain shook his head stubbornly, glaring at his father with a mix of frustration and hurt. The anger inside him was like a storm raging, fueled by years of feeling misunderstood and judged.

"Dad, I'm serious. I need this car. You're the only one who can help me with the cosign," Cain said, his voice tight.

Adam sighed deeply, trying to keep his own emotions in check. "Cain, I know you're upset, son. But I'm just not comfortable co-signing for a car right now. You need to get your priorities straight."

Cain's jaw clenched as he fought to hold back the words burning at the tip of his tongue. "I'm doing everything I can, Dad. I'm working two jobs just to support Cam and the kids."

Adam's expression hardened slightly, a mix of disappointment and resolve washing over his face. "Cain, you made the choice to have three kids. You also made the choice to sell drugs. Your mother and I did everything we could to make sure you and Abel never went without. But you wanted fast money, Cain. When you choose quick cash over an honest living, you have to live with the consequences."

Cain's eyes flashed with resentment. "Yeah, but I bet if Abel asked you to cosign for him, you'd do it without hesitation."

Adam's voice softened, tinged with sadness. "Cain, why do you feel the need to compete with your brother? There's no comparison between you two. I love you just as much as I love him. All your mother and I want is for both of you to love God and live productive, meaningful lives."

He paused, then added firmly, "And for the record, I wouldn't cosign for Abel either. You're both grown men. We gave you the tools you needed to succeed in this world. You can't blame us for the choices you've made."

Cain lowered his head, his pride wounded, anger mixing with shame. The weight of his father's words crushed him in unexpected ways.

Adam reached out, gently squeezing Cain's shoulder. "Son, I'm not trying to hurt you. I just want better for you. You're so smart, Cain. You're gifted beyond measure. God gave you a special gift, and I hate to see you wasting it."

Cain cut him off sharply, his voice cold and distant. "Don't worry about it, Dad. I'll get it on my own."

With that, he stormed out of the house, slamming the door behind him.

Adam stood there, his heart heavy and conflicted. He shook his head slowly, wondering silently where he had gone wrong, and if there was any way to reach the son who was slipping further away.

CHAPTER FIFTEEN

Cain hadn't spoken to his parents since that day three months ago when his father refused to co-sign for his car. The silence between them had grown heavy, thick with frustration and unspoken pain. Now, sitting with his coworkers during lunch at the construction site, Cain's thoughts were far away when the familiar black car rolled up to the entrance.

"I'll be right back," Cain muttered, standing and gathering his lunch as he made his way toward the vehicle.

Abel stepped out, his face hopeful but cautious. "Hey man, it's good to see you," he said softly. "I know you're on your break, but can I talk to you for a few minutes?"

Cain shrugged, trying to mask his tension. "Sure, it's your world, boss man," he replied with a small, forced smile.

Abel sighed deeply, looking Cain in the eyes. "Cain, why does it have to be like this between us? You're my brother.

I love you, and so do Mom and Dad. Why haven't you answered any of their calls?"

Cain's jaw tightened. "For what? To listen to them complain about my life? Or to keep hearing how I should be more like you?"

"It's not like that, Cain. You know it's not. They love you. The least you could do is call and let them know you're okay."

Cain's voice grew colder. "They don't care if I'm okay. They just don't want me to bring any more shame to the family."

"That's not true," Abel insisted. "When you went away, they were devastated. I've never seen Dad cry before—until that day."

Cain's eyes flashed with anger. "Abel, don't come here preaching about calling them. You can pretend whatever you want, but I know the truth. I'm the black sheep of this family."

"Black sheep?" Abel's voice cracked with disbelief. "Cain, what are you talking about? Mom and Dad have always loved us both equally. We've both made mistakes, but that's never stopped their love."

Cain scoffed bitterly. "What mistakes have you made, Mr. Perfect? Since we were kids, you've always been the golden boy. I'm done with it. Like Dad said, I'm a grown man—I don't need any of you."

His voice hardened. "Leave me alone, Abel. Don't come back here."

With that, Cain turned and walked away without looking back.

Abel stood frozen, swallowing the lump in his throat as he watched his brother disappear into the distance. All his life, he had longed for Cain's love and respect. He didn't understand what he had done to deserve this cold rejection. Cain was the most important person in the world to him, and the pain of being pushed away cut deep. Abel glanced back at Cain laughing with his coworkers, a smile that didn't reach his eyes, before the black car pulled away from the site.

As the car disappeared down the road, Abel whispered a silent prayer, hoping that someday Cain would let him back in.

CHAPTER SIXTEEN

Cam couldn't take it anymore. Cain's anger seemed to grow darker and heavier with each passing day, and losing his job only made everything worse. The man she once loved was slipping away from her, swallowed by frustration and bitterness.

"Cain, I love you so much," Cam began, her voice trembling with exhaustion, "but I can't keep doing this. I know things are hard right now, but you act like you're facing it all alone. I'm right here beside you. I've always been here. But I can't keep carrying this weight by myself."

Cain's eyes flashed with resentment. "I can't keep doing this? What exactly am I supposed to be dealing with? I'm the one out there working while you sit around doing nothing."

Cam's breath hitched, hurt and disbelief swirling in her chest. "Are you serious? Sit around? When you came home, I took care of you. I helped you get back on your feet. I'm not working right now because you won't let me be on birth control, and yet you keep getting me pregnant." She stepped closer, her voice breaking with love and frustration. "Cain, I'm not your enemy. I love you. I want you to get yourself together. But I can't live like this anymore. I can't keep letting our children see you like this—they're scared of you."

Cain's face twisted with pain and anger. "Fine. Leave me, just like everyone else does," he spat. "It's like the harder I try, the more y'all condemn me."

"Who, Cain? Who's condemning you?" Cam's voice softened, tears welling in her eyes. "You're surrounded by people who love you—who adore you. But your anger blinds you from seeing it. When you're ready to let go of that anger and really look around, you'll see it's all because we want the best for you. Not for us, not for Mom and Dad, not even for the kids—but for you."

She sat down beside him and gently turned his face toward hers. "Cain, I love you, but I'm scared—so scared. Scared I'll get a call that you were killed driving drunk, or that your anger finally got the best of you. I can't live through you going back to prison. We need you here. I need you here."

Her arms wrapped around him tightly, holding him as the tears spilled down his cheeks.

"I love you, Cam," Cain whispered, voice thick with pain. "But I don't deserve you. There's too much chaos inside me right now. Maybe it's best if you and the kids move back with your parents for a while."

Cam's heart shattered. "Cain, please don't say that."

His voice turned cold. "Please be gone by the time I get back," he said, standing and walking out the door without another word.

Cain made it to his car but couldn't hold back the flood of emotion. He wept openly, a man broken by love and regret.

He loved Cam fiercely, but he felt unworthy—he had already torn apart so much of her life, and he vowed he wouldn't destroy the rest.

Sitting in the car down the street, he watched helplessly as Cam loaded the kids into the truck. The ache in his chest was unbearable. He knew how disappointed both his parents and hers must be.

"God, please help me," he prayed quietly, feeling as if his heart was being ripped from his chest as the truck pulled away.

CHAPTER SEVENTEEN

Cain was sitting alone on the sofa when he heard a knock at the door. He rushed to the door, hoping that Cam had come back. His short-lived hope turned to anger when he saw his brother standing there. What do you want? Cain asked. I just wanted to check on your Cain. Cam called and told us what happened. Cain, you need to get some help. This drinking is getting out of control. I don't want to get a phone call that you hurt yourself or someone else while driving drunk.

Abel, do not walk into my house trying to tell me what to do. As a matter of fact, get out of my house. I told you the last time that I didn't want to see you again. Why can't y'all just leave me alone? Because we love you, Abel yelled. You are my brother, Cain, my twin brother. You are the closest person to me in this world. I love you so much but I don't understand why you hate me so much. What did I do? Ever since we were kids, you treated me like crap. I have always looked up to you. I just want you to love me, Abel cried.

Cain was taken aback for a moment by Abel's outburst. He'd never heard his brother yell before. Cain sat on the couch and put his head down trying to fight back tears threatening to fall. Abel, I don't hate you, he said calmly. I am just tired of living in your shadow.

Abel sat down next to his brother, unsure of how to respond. "Cain, you are my brother, and I love you. I know that things between us have not always been perfect but my love for you has never lessened. I know that things haven't been easy for you the last few years, but I am here and there is nothing that you can so or do to change that." Abel squeezed Cain's shoulder before he stood and left, closing the door quietly behind him.

Cain let the tears fall that he's been fighting to hold back. I love you too, he mumbled as he watched his brother drive away.

CHAPTER EIGHTEEN

Cain thought the pounding he heard was just a fragment of his dream—until he heard his father's voice calling his name softly but insistently. Groaning, he pulled the pillow tighter over his head, took a deep breath, and reluctantly swung his legs off the bed.

He lingered unusually long in the bathroom, washing his face and brushing his teeth with slow, deliberate movements, hoping his father would be gone by the time he emerged. But to his disappointment, Adam was still there, seated quietly on the porch, staring out toward the front door.

Cain took a steadying breath and stepped onto the porch. "I knew you'd answer eventually," Adam said with a gentle smile. Cain said nothing, instead lowering himself onto a chair opposite his father, who rocked slowly in the porch swing.

"I talked to Cameron," Adam began, eyes searching his son's face. "Cain, please... talk to me. Tell me what's going on. You know she loves you with everything she has. She and the kids—they're hurting. They think you're gone because of them. You weren't raised to run away from your responsibilities, son."

Cain's jaw tightened. "Dad, I just need to get myself together. Cam and I—we're constantly fighting. And the kids don't need to see that."

Adam nodded slowly. "What exactly are you two arguing about?"

"Everything," Cain muttered, shaking his head. "Money... it's—" He stopped himself before mentioning the drinking. The last thing he wanted was another lecture about that. He knew he had a problem, but every time he tried to quit, something else fell apart, and the drinking was his only escape.

Adam's gaze sharpened. "Well, son, I'm sure your drinking plays a part in this. I can smell it on you from here. Cain, I love you. I don't want to lose you. You have a problem, and you need help before something worse happens. You're already on the edge of losing your wife and kids forever."

Cain exhaled slowly, struggling to find the words. "Dad, I do everything I can to prove my love to all of you, but it's never enough. I try to be a good husband, a good father, a good son, but it never feels like enough. I cut the grass, fix the cars, help around the house—I do everything you ask."

Tears welled in Adam's eyes as he reached out, resting a firm hand on Cain's shoulder. "Son, you don't have to earn my love. From the moment your mother told me you were growing inside her, I loved you. I don't know why you don't believe that. I love you without conditions. I love you simply because you're my son."

"Why are you so angry?" Adam asked softly. "Have I ever mistreated you? Have I ever given you reason to think I don't love you?"

Cain didn't bother to hide the tears streaming down his face. "Nothing I do is ever enough for you. You make me feel crazy, like I'm imagining things, but you've always treated Abel differently. Even when we were kids, Abel and I would do the same thing, but I was the one who got in trouble."

Adam's expression softened but remained earnest. "Son, those thoughts are lies you tell yourself. Yes, my relationship with Abel is different—but that doesn't mean I love you any less. Cain, you push away everyone who loves you. I've tried to include you, to share things with you and Abel, but you keep shutting us out."

He leaned forward, voice thick with emotion. "I love you because you're my son. I prayed for you and Abel long before you were born. Do you realize all you have to do is

come to me—just as you are? I don't need perfection, Cain.
I just want you. Why do you feel like you have to earn
something that's already yours?"

Cain glanced toward the house, where his alarm was
ringing, reminding him of the day ahead. "I need to get
dressed for work," he said quietly.

Adam stood, pulling his son into a tight embrace. "I love
you, Cain," he whispered, his voice cracking with feeling.
"More than you'll ever know."

CHAPTER NINETEEN

Cain sat on the floor against the wall as his cell phone rang for the third time in the last five minutes. As the tears fell down his face, he looked at his bloodied hands. "Oh my God, I'm so sorry Abel," he cried as he looked at his brother's lifeless body across the room.

Cain slammed his head against the cold, unforgiving wall again and again, each impact echoing the storm raging inside him. His voice cracked as he whispered a desperate prayer, "Please, God... please let this be a nightmare. Just wake me up."

He clenched his eyes shut so tightly it felt like his skull might crack, willing himself to escape this unbearable reality. His chest heaved with ragged breaths, heart pounding as if trying to shatter his ribs. Every nerve screamed for relief, for even the smallest glimmer of hope, but the darkness clung to him like a suffocating shroud.

In that moment, all he wanted was to wake—to break free from the nightmare that had become his life. However, when he opened his eyes all he saw was his brother's lying in the growing pool of blood.

Cain's trembling hands reached out as he crawled across the floor toward his brother's lifeless form. The cold, heavy weight of Abel's body settled into his arms, a cruel reminder of the finality Cain desperately refused to accept. His voice cracked as he whispered through choking sobs, "Father, please forgive me. I'm so sorry… I never wanted this."

He pressed his cheek against Abel's pale skin, feeling the stillness that no heartbeat could break. "Please, Abel… wake up. Please, don't leave me like this," he screamed, his voice raw with pain and disbelief.

Leaning back slowly against the wall, Cain clung to his brother's motionless body as if holding on to the last thread of hope. His arms tightened instinctively, unwilling to let go, while the silence around them pressed down like a suffocating weight.

In that unbearable stillness, all Cain could do was hold on—and pray for a miracle that wouldn't come. Cain spent several minutes staring at the gun that was lying next to him. He picked the gun up off the floor and aimed it at his head after looking over at his brother's bloodied face. I am so sorry God, Cain wept as he pulled the trigger. When Cain heard the gun click and realized it had jammed, he jumped and dropped the gun.

The sharp clatter of the gun hitting the floor shattered the heavy silence, a sound Cain couldn't bear. His anguished scream tore through the air, raw and desperate, echoing off the walls.

Hearing the commotion, Aaron—his next-door neighbor—rushed over, heart pounding in his chest. He froze in horror at the scene before him: Cain, crumpled on the floor, clutching his brother's lifeless body, the gun still clutched loosely in his trembling hand.

Without hesitation, Aaron turned and sprinted back to his house, fumbling for his phone. His fingers trembled as he dialed 911, desperation flooding his voice. "Please, send help—quick. It's an emergency. They need help right now."

As he waited for the paramedics to arrive, Aaron prayed silently, hoping against hope that it wouldn't be too late to save them both.

CHAPTER TWENTY

Adam had been calling Cain repeatedly for the past fifteen minutes, each ring deepening the knot of worry tightening in his chest. It was as if some silent alarm had gone off inside him—an unshakable feeling that something was terribly wrong.

"What's going on?" Eva asked softly, noticing the furrowed lines on her husband's face, the way his eyes darted anxiously toward his phone.

Adam shook his head, trying to mask the growing unease. "I don't know exactly… but I have a bad feeling. Abel went over to check on Cain earlier, but I haven't heard from either of them since. I've been calling for nearly an hour now, and no one is answering."

Eva's voice trembled slightly as she asked, "Should we go over there? Maybe check on them ourselves?"

Adam took a deep breath, steadying himself. "I'll go," he said, forcing calm into his tone, though inside he was anything but. "I'm sure it's probably nothing, but I need to see for myself. Just to be sure."

Eva reached out, squeezing his hand gently. "Okay, baby. Call me as soon as you get there."

"I will. I promise." Adam leaned down and kissed her forehead before grabbing his keys and heading out the door.

Eva watched him go, her heart heavy. She could see the worry etched deep in his face—one she shared. Cain had grown more distant with each passing day. Despite her efforts to reach him since his last visit, her calls went unanswered, swallowed by silence.

As the minutes stretched on, Eva sank to her knees beside the couch, whispering prayers under her breath. *Please, God, keep my boys safe. Don't let them fall apart again. Don't let another fight tear them apart.*

CHAPTER TWENTY-ONE

The sight that met Adam's eyes brought him to his knees, the world seeming to tilt and collapse around him. Time slowed to a painful crawl as he sat frozen, unable to move or breathe. His gaze flickered helplessly between Abel's lifeless body sprawled across the floor and Cain, clutching a gun tightly in his trembling hands.

Summoning every ounce of strength, Adam crawled slowly toward them, his voice trembling with desperation. "Cain… please, give me the gun," he pleaded softly, trying to reach the son he loved beyond all else.

But when Adam looked into Cain's eyes, a cold unfamiliarity gripped his heart. He had seen anger in Cain before, but never such darkness—an unrecognizable shadow of something far more sinister. It was as if Cain had not even registered his father's presence.

"Please, Cain," Adam whispered again, his hand reaching out to gently touch his son's head.

The faintest flinch betrayed Cain's awareness. His eyes shot open, wide and brimming with tears, locking with his father's. The walls Cain had built crumbled in that moment, and sobs racked his body.

"Dad... I'm so sorry," Cain choked out between gasps. "I didn't mean to... I swear."

Adam's own heart shattered, a raw, unbearable pain piercing through him as if a knife had plunged deep into his chest. "My God, Cain... what have you done?" he cried, voice breaking with anguish.

Tenderly, he lifted Cain's face with trembling hands, desperate to bring him back from the edge. "Son, please... give me the gun," he begged once more.

Reluctantly, Cain loosened his grip, handing over the gun with shaking fingers—but he would not release Abel's body. He clung to his brother as though letting go would break the last fragile thread holding him together.

Adam placed the gun gently on the floor, tears streaming down his cheeks as he wrapped his arms around both his boys—one silent, one shattered.

"Father… I need you," Cain whispered, his voice raw and broken.

Adam's shirt grew soaked—not just with his own tears, but with the mingled sorrow and pain of his sons, a heartbreaking testament to a family on the brink. And in that moment, all Adam could do was hold them both, praying for a mercy he desperately hoped would come.

CHAPTER TWENTY-TWO

Adam was utterly exhausted. After hours of restless tossing and turning, the possibility of sleep had long since slipped away. His mind was a storm of swirling thoughts, and his heart felt unbearably heavy—like a weight crushing his very soul. Eventually, he pushed back the covers and silently slipped out of bed, careful not to wake Eva.

He made his way to the living room and sank into his worn recliner, his gaze immediately drawn to the family portrait hanging over the mantle. The photograph captured a moment frozen in time—his boys when they were just two years old, smiling brightly with innocence and promise. Adam's eyes welled with tears as he squeezed them shut, the ache in his chest tightening like a vise.

He struggled to block out the painful memory of walking into the house, drenched in Abel's blood. It had taken Eva a moment to realize the blood wasn't Adam's. But the look on his face—ashen and broken—said everything without a single word spoken. Without hesitation, Eva had dropped to her knees and wept, her sobs echoing the grief that consumed them both.

The evening had slipped away in a haze of prayer and tears. Adam's mind replayed the image of Eva, subconsciously rubbing her stomach, a gesture so familiar—one she'd made the day they discovered she was pregnant with twins. That small moment of joy now felt like a cruel reminder of everything they had lost.

There had been tension between Cain and Abel for some time, Adam knew that. But never, not in his wildest nightmares, had he imagined it would end like this—so sudden, so devastating.

In the blink of an eye, they had lost not one, but both their sons.

Adam bowed his head, whispering a prayer for strength and mercy. He prayed for the courage to endure this unfathomable pain, to hold onto hope when all seemed lost.

With a heavy heart, he rose from the recliner and quietly

moved to check on Eva, knowing they would need each

other more than ever in the days to come.

CHAPTER TWENTY-THREE

The morning of Cain's sentencing was heavy with gloom. A thick, gray sky hung low, matching the weight in Eva and Adam's hearts. They were quietly grateful that the trial had been avoided—Cain's guilty plea sparing them the ordeal of a prolonged legal battle—but that small mercy did little to ease the ache. Adam dreaded the moment he would see his son walk into the courtroom in handcuffs. It still felt surreal, like a nightmare they couldn't wake from. Nearly a year had passed, but the pain remained as raw as the day it happened.

Adam's mind drifted back to Abel's funeral—a bittersweet reminder of a life cut tragically short. He'd never fully realized just how many lives Abel had touched: the children he mentored, the men's group for husbands and fathers he passionately led at church. In just thirty brief years, Abel had accomplished more than many do in a lifetime. Yet now, they would never know the full measure of his potential, nor the dreams he still held.

Adam took a slow, steadying breath and reached out, gently squeezing Eva's hand. Anger still churned within him like a storm he couldn't calm. *"Lord, please help me,"* he silently prayed. *"I love my son, but I am overwhelmed with rage. How could he do this—hurt his own brother? Please, grant me the strength to forgive."*

Beside him, Eva sat quietly, tears slipping down her cheeks. She closed her eyes, her hand resting instinctively on her belly, rubbing it absentmindedly. For the past year, she had prayed for understanding, wrestling with a grief that felt impossible to bear. After years of longing and hoping, she had finally become pregnant—only to have one son take the life of the other.

Eva had never questioned God before, but now, doubt gnawed at her heart. Did she not love Cain enough? Was there something she had done, some mistake she had made, that led them here? Her thoughts shattered the moment Cain was led into the courtroom.

She hadn't seen him since his first court appearance. The sight of him made her heart break anew. Cain had lost so much weight; the light in his eyes dimmed, replaced by something raw and haunted. As furious as she was with him, he was still her son. And no matter the pain he had caused, she loved him fiercely.

People always assumed Abel was the sensitive one, but Eva knew otherwise. Cain had always worn his heart on his sleeve, taking everything personally, while Abel had a quiet way of compartmentalizing his feelings. Even as children, Cain had craved the spotlight, demanding attention, while Abel preferred to fade into the background. She wished she could go back, to find a sign—anything—that this tragedy was coming.

Adam leaned close and whispered softly into her ear, "It's okay." But the words barely touched the fear and sorrow that made her shiver—one son killing the other was a pain

too deep to put into words.

CHAPTER TWENTY-FOUR

Cain paced relentlessly back and forth in the small, cold cell, the dull concrete walls closing in on him. His heart hammered against his ribs as he waited for the guard to call his name. Two weeks ago, he had received a letter from his father. His hands had trembled so violently that he struggled just to read the words. The letter had brought news he wasn't sure he was ready for—his parents were coming to visit him.

Cain hadn't seen or spoken to them since the day of his sentencing, nearly three years ago. The memory of that day lingered like a heavy fog, impossible to shake. For the first eleven months of his five-year sentence, he had been confined to the psychiatric ward, his mind tormented by relentless visions of Abel. Those haunting images never faded—the moment his brother collapsed, the final words Abel spoke echoing in his ears: "I love you."

His hands still shook as he tried to steady them, an instinctive urge to avoid the inevitable. He didn't want to see his parents—the way their eyes would darken with hurt, anger, and disappointment. Yet beneath the fear, he knew they deserved closure. They needed to understand, to find some peace, even if he was far from finding any himself. Cain's guilt was a heavy, suffocating weight. He had never meant to kill Abel. The memories were fragmented, hauntingly incomplete. He didn't recall picking up the gun or pulling the trigger—only the shattering moment when his brother fell to the floor and whispered those last words of love. It was that bittersweet confession that made the guilt impossible to escape.

Suddenly, the nausea overwhelmed him. Cain bolted to the toilet and vomited violently, his body wracked with pain and regret. He wiped his mouth with trembling hands and slowly slid down to sit against the cold wall, closing his eyes and drawing in a shaky breath to calm the storm inside him.

He had been the family's troublemaker for years—multiple arrests, reckless decisions, DUIs—but none of that compared to this. This was beyond anything he could have imagined or forgiven himself for. The consequences of his actions had shattered his family, leaving scars deeper than any prison walls.

Despite the fear twisting in his gut, Cain knew he had to face his parents. He had to summon every ounce of strength to confront the past and do what was right—whatever that meant now.

CHAPTER TWENTY-FIVE

Eva sat quietly at the small kitchen table, her fingers twisting nervously as she wrung her hands. The room felt unbearably still, charged with the weight of years and unspoken pain. She hadn't seen Cain in so long—years since his sentencing—and the thought of facing him again filled her with a whirlwind of conflicting emotions. Uncertainty gnawed at her, but beneath it all was a steady, unshakable truth: he was her son, and no matter what had happened, she loved him deeply.

Abel's death had shattered her world. The grief was raw and relentless, cutting to her very core. Every day without Abel felt like a wound reopening. Yet, Eva was determined—she refused to let the darkness steal away the rest of her family. She would not let the devil rob her of both sons.

She knew Cain better than anyone. Despite their history, despite the jealousy Cain had harbored since childhood,

Eva believed with every fiber of her being that Cain would never have harmed Abel if his mind had been clear. Cain's love for his brother had always been complicated but real. It was a love that, she hoped, still lingered beneath the guilt and regret.

Eva reached out and gently rubbed Adam's hand, sensing the tension in his fingers as he drummed nervously on the table. She smiled softly at him, trying to infuse some calm into the room. "I love you," she said quietly.

Adam returned her smile, leaning over to kiss her hand before letting out a heavy sigh. Eva always had a way of soothing his worries, grounding him when the weight of their shared grief felt unbearable. He missed both of his sons profoundly, the ache a constant presence in his heart. Yet he was grateful—grateful that Cam and Leslie, the women who had stood by their family, remained close, offering a lifeline through their shared pain. The grandchildren, too, were a source of comfort; their laughter and resilience brought moments of light into the darkness. Adam also found solace in the unexpected strength their family had discovered. The tragedy that might have torn them apart had instead drawn them closer. Cam had been devastated when Adam told her about Abel's death. She carried a heavy burden of guilt, blaming herself for leaving Cain and fearing she had pushed him to the edge. But Leslie, Abel's wife, refused to let that guilt consume them. She reminded Cam—and everyone—that some things were beyond their control.

Before Abel's death, Leslie and Cam hadn't spent much time together, their relationship limited by circumstance and distance. But now, united by shared heartbreak and the fragile hope of healing, they had become inseparable. Leslie was the sister Cam never had, and together they made sure the children stayed connected, weaving a web of support that held the family together.

It hadn't been easy at first. The older children struggled with the loss and the complicated emotions tied to Cain. But over time, they found strength in each other. What the enemy had intended to destroy their family only made them stronger, more united than ever before.

CHAPTER TWENTY-SIX

Cain's heart pounded so loudly he was sure the entire corridor could hear it as he followed the officer down the cold, sterile hallway toward the visitor's room. Every step felt heavier than the last, weighed down by years of regret and longing. All Cain had ever wanted was the approval of his parents—their unconditional love and acceptance that had always seemed just out of reach. He shook his head, trying to banish the dark, negative thoughts clawing at his mind, but they lingered stubbornly as they neared the room. Ahead, he saw the unmistakable silhouette of his father—tall, broad-shouldered, and seemingly immovable. Panic surged through Cain's chest, tightening its grip. His breath hitched. The officer noticed immediately and gently asked, "Are you okay?"

"No," Cain sobbed, his voice breaking. "I can't do this." He took a step back, his hands trembling as he tried to retreat from the visitor's room entrance.

The older officer raised a hand and nodded, signaling for the younger guard to give them some privacy. He crouched down beside Cain, his voice soft but firm. "Cain, I know this is hard. Really hard. But you owe it to them—and to yourself—to try. I have four kids at home, and I can't imagine what it would be like to go through what your family has endured. Your parents deserve closure."

Tears spilled down Cain's cheeks as he whispered, "I know… but I'm scared to see the hurt I caused them."

The officer gave a small, reassuring nod. "Cain, listen to me—parental love isn't something you have to earn. It's given freely, without conditions. No matter what you've done, your parents still love you. I'm willing to bet they've already forgiven you."

Cain shook his head, despair thick in his voice. "The hardest part is forgiving myself."

"I know," the officer replied quietly. "You hurt your brother, and that's a wound you'll carry for a long time.

But I'm sure Abel has forgiven you too. That's why we have to keep praying. The enemy waits for the smallest crack in our faith, one moment of weakness, and that's when lives can be torn apart."

Cain closed his eyes, heart aching, wishing desperately he could rewind time and undo the nightmare of that day. For so many years, he'd tried to put distance between himself and his parents, to avoid the pain of rejection. Now, more than anything, he just wanted to be near them—to feel some semblance of home.

The officer's voice broke through his thoughts again. "Are you ready now?"

Cain inhaled deeply, the air burning his lungs, but he nodded. "Yes."

"Good," the officer said, standing and placing a steady hand on Cain's shoulder. "Now, pull yourself together. This is your chance to begin healing. You can do this."

With trembling hands, Cain wiped away his tears, squared his shoulders, and stepped into the visiting room—ready, at last, to face the family he had so longed to reconcile with.

CHAPTER TWENTY-SEVEN

Cain's legs trembled uncontrollably as his gaze remained fixed on the table before him. The weight of everything pressed down so heavily that he could barely breathe. "Son, lift your head," Adam's voice was gentle but firm, breaking through the silence.

At the sound of his father calling him "son," Cain's composure crumbled. Tears spilled down his face as he began to weep again. "Hold your head up, son," Adam repeated softly, his eyes filled with compassion and sorrow. Swallowing the lump that caught in his throat, Cain finally met his father's gaze. "I'm so sorry," he choked out between sobs. "I never meant for any of this to happen. I don't know what went wrong."

Eva closed her eyes, whispering a silent prayer for strength. When she finally spoke, her voice was tender but resolute. "We know that, Cain. We know you loved your brother. Yes, you two had your differences—like any siblings—but at the end of the day, your love for Abel was real. And Abel loved you."

Cain's voice cracked as he struggled to speak. "I know you hate me, and I'm so sorry for... I wish I could take his place. I don't understand how it happened. One moment we were arguing, and the next, there was blood everywhere."

Eva fought back a sob and straightened her back. She didn't need to hear the painful details again. What she knew, what broke her heart every day, was that she had lost both of her sons. Cain and Abel were very different boys, but they were both her sons—and she loved them deeply.

Slowly, Eva stretched her trembling hand across the table and took Cain's hand in hers. "We forgive you, Cain," she said quietly but firmly. "We forgive you, and we love you. We know you would never have intentionally hurt your brother."

Her eyes glistened with tears as she continued, "Now, I ask that you forgive us—your mother and me. Forgive us for anything we did that made you feel you weren't enough. We love you very much, Cain. We always have, and nothing you do can change that."

Her voice broke, but she pressed on. "I'm heartbroken and disappointed, yes. But my love for you will never waver—not until my last breath. The devil has already stolen one of my sons. I will not let him take you too."

"I don't deserve your forgiveness," Cain sobbed, his voice raw with anguish. "I just want to die. I killed my brother," he said, clenching his teeth to hold back a scream building inside him. "I wished they had given me the death penalty like I asked."

Adam shook his head gently, his voice steady but filled with sorrow. "What would that have solved? It wouldn't have brought Abel back. It would've only caused more pain for your mother and me. We truly love you, Cain. You're all we have left, and we refuse to lose you too."

"We will get through this—as a family," Adam continued. "Honor your brother by living your best life. Abel believed in you, just as your mother and I do. And I believe that God will turn this tragedy around. But you still must face the consequences of what happened." Cain nodded, tears still flowing.

"We need you, son. And so do your children. They miss you."

Cain's voice cracked again. "I don't deserve to have them in my life."

"If God gave everyone what they deserved," Eva said softly, "we'd all be in trouble."

Adam offered a faint glimmer of hope. "The lawyer told us there's a good chance our request for early probation will be granted. Son, you need to find a way to forgive yourself. If you don't, the guilt will consume you."

Adam's voice softened as he reflected. "I've been wrestling with guilt myself. Looking back, there are moments with you and Abel I wish I'd handled differently."

"Cain, you are my son—flesh of my flesh, blood of my blood. I loved you before I even knew you."

Cain lowered his head onto the table, overwhelmed by grief. Adam's voice came again, full of earnest love. "All your mother and I ever wanted was for you and your brother to be happy. Not once, not for a single moment, did we stop loving you. We may have been disappointed by some choices you made, but our love never lessened."

Adam's voice cracked as he added, "I don't know what we did to make you feel otherwise, but we are truly sorry."

Eva reached out, her voice gentle but hopeful. "We all need a fresh start. When you come home, your father and I want you to move back in for a while—until you get back on your feet. We could all use some time together."

Cain shook his head, fear tightening his throat. "Dad, I can't... I can't go back into that house. There are too many memories."

Adam reached across and squeezed his son's shoulder. "Son, sometimes memories can be a good thing. We need to get through this—together. It won't be easy for any of us, but we are family. And we will make it through."

CHAPTER TWENTY-EIGHT

Three months later, Cain received the news he had been waiting for—his parole was granted, just as his attorney had promised. But the freedom he longed for didn't feel like a gift; it felt undeserved. His heart was heavy with the knowledge that his brother was still gone—gone forever—and that it was his fault. No matter how much time passed or what he did, Cain could not find a way to forgive himself.

He knew, deep down, that Abel had always been the better man between them. Despite their constant fights, Cain couldn't imagine a world where Abel no longer existed. The thought of a life without his brother was unbearable. As they drove home, Adam glanced at Cain through the rearview mirror. "What's on your mind, son?" Cain's voice was quiet, almost fragile. "I was just thinking about Abel. We fought so much growing up—I used to wish I could just move somewhere no one knew I was a twin. But now... all I want is to be with him."

Adam chuckled softly, trying to lighten the mood. "I remember feeling the same way when your aunt Angie was born. Your grandmother said whenever your sister and I fought, I'd cry and beg them to take her back to the hospital."

He smiled, then grew more serious. "All siblings go through that phase. I imagine it's even harder when you're identical twins, both trying to find your own identity."

Adam reached over and gave Cain's shoulder a reassuring squeeze. "I know for a fact that you got on Abel's nerves just as much as he got on yours. But that's family, son. We're not always going to get along, but we stand together—no matter what."

Cain's voice hardened with anger. "How? How can you and Mom still stand with me after what I did? I killed him. I killed my own brother."

Eva flinched at the words, closing her eyes to steady herself before she spoke. "Cain, we stand with you because you are our son. God loves us unconditionally. If He can love without limits, who are we to put restrictions on our love for you?"

Her voice trembled with raw emotion. "You broke my heart, Cain. Losing Abel was the hardest thing I have ever had to endure. No parent should ever outlive their child. Hate… hate is easy. It's easy to hate someone who has hurt you deeply."

"But loving beyond the pain—that's the hard part. Loving someone who tore your heart out is one of the hardest things you will ever do. But I made a choice to love you from the moment the doctor told me I was carrying you and your brother in my womb. And I will keep loving you until the day I take my last breath."

Eva paused, swallowing the lump in her throat. "For days after it happened, I couldn't speak. I kept asking myself what I did—or didn't do—to prevent this. But the truth is, as much as it hurts, there was nothing I could have done to stop it. I don't know why God chose to take Abel home when He did, but He did—and that is something we all must accept."

Her voice carried to the backseat, filled with both sorrow and strength. "Beating yourself up won't bring Abel back, Cain. You have to find a way to live with this pain—and someday, maybe even find forgiveness for yourself."

CHAPTER TWENTY-NINE

The next few months proved far harsher than Cain had ever imagined. The crushing weight of guilt pressed down on him relentlessly, suffocating him with every breath. Though he was technically free, he felt trapped inside a prison of his own making—a cage forged from regret and self-loathing. Forgiving himself felt impossible, and every day was a battle against the voices that whispered he didn't deserve the second chance he'd been given.

Cain kept to himself, doing everything in his power to stay out of his parents' way. He threw himself into work and cherished the limited moments he had with his children, desperately clinging to whatever fragments of normalcy he could salvage. But the cracks in his resolve showed in heartbreaking ways—like the day his young daughter, innocent and confused, asked him quietly, "Daddy, why did you kill Uncle Abel?"

He closed his eyes, swallowing the lump in his throat as tears threatened to spill. The question reopened wounds he had tried so hard to bury.

His mind drifted back to one night in particular—a night that had etched itself into his soul. He had quietly walked into the den, only to find his mother curled into a fetal position on the couch, her body trembling with sobs. Clutched tightly in her hands was Abel's law school graduation photo, the very image of a future that would never be.

Cain had wanted to reach out, to offer some fragile comfort, but the guilt was a chain wrapped so tightly around his heart that he froze. He was the source of her anguish, the cause of this unbearable pain—and he knew, with painful certainty, that he was the last person she wanted to see.

Silently, he retreated, escaping to the solitude of his own room. The ache of seeing his mother so broken was unbearable. He hated himself for the devastation he'd wrought, and that hatred nearly swallowed him whole. The sickness that had been building inside him erupted, and Cain barely made it to the bathroom in time. He doubled over the toilet, tears streaming down his face, body wracked with sobs. His head rested against the cold porcelain as memories flooded his mind—the laughter and warmth of their childhood together. Birthday parties filled with balloons and cake, Christmas mornings wrapped in joy and wonder. Those moments felt impossibly distant now.

Despite the pain, a faint smile touched his lips as he clung to those memories, even as he knew life would never be the same. No matter how many times his parents told him they forgave him, the truth remained: Cain would forever carry the weight of what he had done.

Eventually, he flushed the toilet and rose to his feet, his movements slow and heavy. He washed his hands, brushed his teeth, and then—without thinking—walked to his parents' bedroom. There, on the nightstand, sat a bottle of sleeping pills. He took it without hesitation.

Back in his room, he locked the door behind him and swallowed the pills one by one, feeling their cold presence slide down his throat. The drowsiness came swiftly, a seductive escape from the torment.

As the darkness crept in, Cain whispered a final prayer, voice trembling with sorrow and regret: "Father, I cannot bear the agony of the pain I have caused my family. Please forgive me for what I am about to do."

And with that, he surrendered to the sleep that threatened to swallow him whole.

CHAPTER THIRTY

Eva sat up abruptly on the couch, wiping the hot tears streaming down her cheeks. A cold, unsettling feeling gnawed at her chest—an uneasiness she couldn't shake. Her breath caught, and she whispered to herself, steadying her trembling voice: "My Father did not give me a spirit of fear, but of power, love and a sound mind."

With resolve flickering in her eyes, she rose and moved silently through the dimly lit house. The quiet was heavy, almost suffocating. Approaching Cain's door, she paused, her hand trembling slightly before she knocked softly.

"Cain, it's me," she called gently, her voice laced with concern.

No answer.

She knocked again, more lightly this time, then cautiously pushed the door open.

Inside, Cain lay motionless on the bed, clutching an old photograph—himself and Abel on their very first

Christmas, their young faces frozen in time and innocence. Eva's heart clenched as she stepped further into the room, but then her gaze dropped to the floor—and froze.

There, lying discarded and ominously empty, was the pill bottle.

A chill swept through her body as her hands began to tremble uncontrollably. She knelt, picking up the bottle with a shaking hand, and the realization crashed over her like a tidal wave. "No, no, no!" she screamed, the sound shattering the stillness of the house.

Panic propelled her to the phone. Fingers fumbling, she dialed 911, her voice breaking as she prayed through tears, "Please God, I cannot lose another son... not now, not like this."

As the operator's calm but urgent instructions filtered through the receiver, Eva's hands worked frantically to perform CPR on Cain. "Cain! What were you thinking?

Stay with me, son! Please!" she cried, her voice raw and desperate, each second stretching endlessly in agony. The world around her narrowed to that small, dim room— the sound of her own ragged breathing, the echo of the operator's voice, and the fragile hope that Cain's heart would beat again.

CHAPTER THIRTY-ONE

Cain's eyelids fluttered open slowly, the harsh glare of the hospital lights forcing him to squint. The sterile white ceiling came into focus before his gaze shifted left—to find his parents standing quietly by his bedside, their faces etched with exhaustion and worry. To his right, Cam and Leslie stood, their expressions a mixture of relief and lingering fear.

A bitter thought crept into Cain's mind: *I can't even kill myself right.* His body ached fiercely, a sharp pain radiating through his chest as he tried to lift himself up. A wince escaped him, and he reluctantly sank back down onto the hospital bed.

Adam's voice broke the heavy silence. "The doctors spent over thirty minutes trying to bring you back, son." His tone was steady but filled with a deep, aching relief.

Cain reached out and gently brushed his mother's hair as she leaned into his side, tears streaming freely down her cheeks. "Momma, I'm sorry," Cain choked out, voice cracking. "I wasn't trying to hurt you... I thought this would make things easier for everyone."

Eva's eyes snapped open, her face hardening as she steadied herself against the weight of his words. "Cain," she said, her voice trembling with a mix of anger and heartbreak, "how could you think that dying would make anything easier for me? I buried one son once already!" Her voice cracked as she shouted, the rawness of her pain filling the room. "You keep telling us you want to make things easier, but let me tell you this—if you want to make me happy, live your life to the fullest, the best way your God-given strength allows."

Eva's voice softened, yet each word carried the weight of years of love and loss. "Be the man of God your father and I prayed you and Abel would become. Be the amazing father your children deserve. Cain, be the husband Cam deserves."

Cam wiped her tears silently, her fingers trembling as Leslie gently rubbed her shoulders. Eva continued, "You're not fighting this battle alone, Cain. Cam has stood by you through everything—prison sentences, DUIs, and yes, even the times you thought she didn't know about those other women." Cam's lips pressed tightly together as a painful truth settled in the room. "You were so lost in your own hurt; you never saw her pain."

Turning Cain's face toward her with tender insistence, Eva's eyes locked on his. "Son, I love you. But it's time to grow up and step into the man God made you to be. You don't owe your father and me anything except to be the man we raised you to be. And Cain—if you ever try something like this again," she said, pulling a belt from her purse and raising it lightly with a sharp look, "your chest won't be the only thing hurting."

A faint laugh escaped from Cam and Leslie, memories flashing of the spankings Eva and Adam had given them all as kids—discipline met with love and tough grace.

In that moment, amidst the pain and tension, a fragile hope blossomed—perhaps this was the turning point Cain needed to finally face his future with courage.

CHAPTER THIRTY-TWO

Bill Withers' *Just the Two of Us* gently drifted from the speakers of Adam's '67 metallic blue Impala as it rolled slowly along the busy stretch of I-295. Cain sat quietly in the passenger seat, eyes closed tightly, trying to push away the flood of memories—memories of simpler, happier times. He remembered how, when Cain and Abel were young, Adam would sing that song, changing the lyrics with a laugh to *Just the Three of Us*.

"How are you feeling, son?" Adam asked softly, glancing over at Cain.

"I've been better," Cain murmured, his voice low and raw—reminding Adam of the times Cain had been in trouble as a boy.

"Cain, I really think you should talk to someone," Adam pressed gently.

Cain nodded, not wanting to argue. He didn't think he needed a psychiatrist—what he truly needed was to pay for his sins. Forgiveness felt out of reach, and therapy seemed like an empty gesture.

As they pulled up to his parents' home, Cain spotted Cam sitting quietly on the porch with his mother. Both women stood when Adam and Cain stepped out of the car.

"Hi, Cam," Cain said without stopping, his voice flat. She was the last person he wanted to see.

If he was honest with himself, Cain had always loved Cam—but he couldn't give her what she needed. Living at his parents' house with no job, no car, and a criminal record made him feel like a failure. He didn't want her pity.

"Hi, Ma," he muttered, avoiding eye contact as he walked past his mother. He'd heard she was the one who had found him and performed CPR. The last thing Cain wanted was to face the people he had tried so hard to escape.

"Wait right here," Eva said to Cam before following Cain into the house, stopping him just before he reached his bedroom.

"We need to talk, son."

"Ma, I don't mean to be disrespectful, but I don't want to talk about it."

"Well, that's too bad," her voice cracked. Cain sighed and took the chair farthest from her.

"Son, I can't imagine the pain you must have been in to do something like that."

"I just wanted to make things right, Ma," Cain whispered, voice breaking. "I should be the one dead, not Abel. He was a better man than I'll ever be, and he didn't deserve to die. You shouldn't have to suffer by looking at me every day."

Eva took a breath. "Cain, let me ask you—out of all your children, which one is your favorite?"

"I don't have a favorite, Ma. I love all my kids the same."

"That's not true," she said softly. "You must have a favorite."

"No, Ma. I love all my kids equally. I'd give my life for all of them. I don't have a favorite."

Eva smiled sadly. "Then tell me this—why do you think I'd love Abel more than I love you? When I found out I was pregnant with you and your brother, I'd given up hope of having children. I was scared the entire time I carried you. I prayed every day for God to protect you both because I loved you before I ever saw your faces."

She reached out, touching his hand gently. "Cain, I love you just as much as I loved your brother. This—this was a trick from the enemy, trying to tear us apart. He wanted you to die, but I declare in the name of Jesus that you will live and not die. You are my son, and God says if I live right, He will protect my seed."

Cain's eyes filled with tears.

"I forgive you, son. I know how much you loved your brother. I won't let this destroy our family. I will love you until the day I take my last breath. Nothing will ever change that."

Cain lowered his head, tears streaming down his cheeks. "Ma, I never meant to hurt anyone. Not you, not Dad. It's just… I've always felt like I wasn't good enough."

She squeezed his hand. "Tell me."

"I remember when Abel got hit by that car years ago. I know it was my fault. But Ma, I swear I never meant for him to get hurt. After that, word spread around the neighborhood. People started calling me the black sheep of the family. I didn't even know what that meant at the time, but when I grew up and understood, that's exactly how I felt."

Cain's voice cracked. "I stopped caring about making you and Dad proud. If I'm honest, it made me rebel more. The more you praised Abel, the angrier I became. I loved him, but I resented him too."

Tears welled in Eva's eyes as she pulled Cain close. "Baby, don't you think I know that? There are no black sheep in this family. I wish you knew just how much I love you. Yes, you were a handful growing up, but you were my handful. Nothing you could ever do would make me stop loving you. You are my pride and joy. There is no life without you."

She looked him firmly in the eyes. "I have already lost one son. Please promise me you'll never do anything like this again."

Cain nodded, voice breaking. "Ma, I never meant to hurt you. But when I saw you in the den that night, I realized just how much pain I caused. I wish I could take it back, but I can't. Every day I wake up to the nightmare of knowing I killed my brother and pushed everyone away."

Eva's expression softened. "Son, no matter what you do, you can never push your father or me away. This isn't easy, and it may take time, but we will get through this—

together. You are going to have to forgive yourself. I wish I could take that hurt away, but only God can do that."

Cain's voice was barely a whisper. "Ma, how can God forgive me? I killed my brother."

Eva smiled with a gentle strength. "He forgives the same way Jesus forgave those who crucified Him. God doesn't require understanding, only faith."

She opened the door and motioned toward Cam. "Now, you need to talk to your wife."

CHAPTER THIRTY-THREE

"Hi," Cam said softly, her voice trembling as she fought back tears. Her heart ached for Cain—she understood all too well the fierce anger he harbored toward Abel, but she also knew deep down that Cain would never have intentionally hurt his brother.

"How are you?" she asked gently, searching his face.

Cain managed a small, weary smile. "I've been better."

Cam's eyes glistened with relief. "I'm so glad you're okay. I don't know what I would've done if something had happened to you. I love you, Cain. I always have."

A faint smile touched Cain's lips. "I know."

After a pause, Cain asked quietly, "Do the kids know?"

Cam shook her head, her voice tender but firm. "No, I didn't want to worry them."

"Thank you," Cain murmured, swallowing hard. "I'm sorry I scared you."

Cam reached out, squeezing his hand gently. "You don't owe me an apology. All I want is for you to be okay. I'm here, Cain. I will always be here."

Cain looked away for a moment, gathering his thoughts. Then, his voice wavered as he asked the question that had been weighing on his mind for months: "Then why did you file for divorce?"

Cam's eyes filled with a mixture of sadness and resolve. "Cain, I will love you until the day I take my last breath. I do love you. But sometimes… your temper frightens me."

Cain's face crumpled with pain. "I would never hurt—" He stopped himself, tears spilling down his cheeks. "I guess… I am capable of hurting the ones I love the most," he admitted, voice breaking.

Without hesitation, Cam moved closer and wrapped her arms around him. Cain leaned into her embrace, letting the tears fall freely as the weight of his guilt and grief poured out.

"I'm not scared of you hurting me," she whispered gently, brushing a tear from his cheek. "Even after everything, that's never been a fear. What worries me is the example it sets for the kids. I don't want them to think this behavior is normal, because it isn't."

She looked into his eyes with unwavering love. "You are my first and only love, Cain. I will love you whether we're together or not."

Silence hung between them for several minutes before Cain finally spoke, voice barely above a whisper. "I don't want to lose you."

Cam smiled softly, a spark of hope flickering in her eyes. "Then we have a lot of work to do. Because we can't keep going like this."

Cain nodded slowly. "I know."

"I know," Cam echoed, holding him a little tighter.

CHAPTER THIRTY-FOUR

Cain had shifted in his seat more times than he could count over the last five minutes, his fingers tapping nervously against his thigh. The sterile walls of Dr. Gray's office seemed to close in on him, the silence heavy and uncomfortable.

"Are you okay, Mr. Jamison?" Dr. Gray asked gently, his tone calm and inviting.

Cain hesitated before answering honestly, his voice low and strained. "Not really. I'm not used to talking about my feelings."

Dr. Gray nodded with understanding. "Well, think of this more as a conversation. Let me start." He took a breath, then shared his story. "I went to school on a football scholarship. During practice, I scrambled to recover a fumble and collided head-on with a teammate. I had surgery to stabilize my spine, but I was never able to play again. That's why I limp."

Cain glanced down at his own hands as the doctor continued. "Two weeks later, my father killed himself. He didn't leave a note, so part of me always wonders if it had anything to do with my injury—if I'd somehow ruined his dream of having a son in the NFL."

The doctor's voice softened. "I shared these feelings with my mom after the funeral, and she told me about his struggles with mental health—how much he loved us but refused to get help. It was then I decided to study psychology."

Cain looked up, curious now. "Why psychology?"

Dr. Gray smiled gently. "Because men—especially black men—are often told that crying or showing emotion makes us weak. So instead of seeking help when life gets overwhelming, many turn to alcohol, drugs, or worse. I got tired of watching men like my father fall because of that stigma." He looked at Cain, encouragingly. "Your turn."

Cain swallowed hard, the words catching in his throat. "I...
I killed my twin brother." He waited for a reaction, but Dr.
Gray remained composed, silently urging him to continue.
"Growing up, I always felt like Abel was the favorite. My
parents never said it outright, but it was a feeling that ate at
me. Over time, my resentment grew. I think I even hated
him. And now, all I can think about is how much I loved
him."

His voice cracked. "He never turned his back on me. Even
when I was mean, he treated me with love and respect. No
matter how angry I got, I never thought about... killing
him. I don't even remember what we argued about that
day."

Dr. Gray's voice was gentle but direct. "Do you remember
pulling the trigger?"

Cain visibly flinched at the word. Tears welled up and
began to spill down his cheeks. "No... I don't. I didn't even

own a gun. I was holding it for a friend who didn't want it around his kids. I'd never even held a gun before that day."

"Take me back to that day," the doctor urged softly. "I know it's hard, but take your time."

Cain closed his eyes, trying to piece together the shattered fragments of memory. "He came over to talk about visiting our parents. I was angry with them. I hadn't called or visited in a while. We started arguing. After that, I don't remember much... just my dad telling me to give him the gun... and the blood. So much blood."

He shivered, reliving the trauma.

CHAPTER THIRTY-FIVE

Surprisingly, Cain felt lighter as he stepped out of Dr. Gray's office, like a single breath of peace had finally pushed its way through the fog that had wrapped itself around his chest for so long. For the first time in what felt like forever, there was a flicker of something in his chest— a quiet, cautious hope. It was small, almost fragile, but it was there. He had made a promise to return next week, and to Cain's own surprise, he intended to keep it.

As he stepped into the elevator and pressed the button for the ground floor, Cain leaned back against the wall and let out a long, tired sigh. The session had drained him emotionally, but it had also left him feeling—alive. More aware. Like he had finally spoken out loud a truth he'd been choking on for years.

The elevator doors slid open with a soft chime, and he took one slow step forward before freezing in place. There she was.

Leslie.

She stood just ahead of him, her hair swept into a neat bun,
her dark sunglasses pulled down from her face. Her eyes
met his without flinching. She didn't look angry, but she
didn't look forgiving either. Her expression was
unreadable, but her presence alone caused Cain's stomach
to tighten.

"Hi, Cain," she said, her voice low, almost fragile.

Cain felt his breath catch in his throat. He nodded, unable
to form a proper response. He dropped his gaze to the tiled
floor, ashamed. Of what he'd done. Of what he'd taken. Of
how much her face reminded him of the man he missed
every second of every day.

"I told your dad I'd pick you up," she continued, her voice
firmer now, but not unkind. "I think it's time we talked,
don't you?"

Cain swallowed hard, his jaw clenched tight. Every fiber of
his being wanted to retreat back into the safety of Dr.

Gray's office—somewhere where he didn't have to face the wreckage he had caused. Somewhere where he wasn't forced to look into the eyes of someone whose life he'd shattered.

Still, he nodded. Not because he was ready—but because he owed her this.

Leslie gave a small nod of her own and turned without another word. "Let's grab a cup of coffee and talk," she said over her shoulder, walking toward the exit without waiting for his response.

Cain followed slowly, each step heavy with dread. His heart pounded in his chest. Conversations like this didn't come with a script. There were no rehearsals, no rewrites. Just truth. Raw and painful.

As they exited the building, the late afternoon sun cast long shadows on the pavement. Cain blinked against the brightness, grateful for the distraction of the light. He kept his eyes on Leslie's heels as she led the way across the parking lot to her car—a silver crossover SUV he remembered Abel had picked out for her on their tenth anniversary.

The drive to the coffee shop was mostly quiet, filled with the soft hum of the engine and the occasional sound of Leslie adjusting the air conditioner. Cain kept his hands clasped tightly in his lap, eyes fixed on the passing trees outside the window, his mind racing with all the possible ways their conversation could go.

When they arrived, Leslie parked and stepped out without a word. Cain followed her inside the quiet, nearly empty café. The barista, a young woman with purple hair and a tired smile, greeted them. Leslie ordered two coffees— black for Cain, hazelnut latte for herself—and led them to a small booth tucked into the back corner.

Cain sat stiffly across from her, the steam from the coffee curling between them like fog on a battlefield. He stared at the cup but didn't touch it. His hands trembled slightly, so he kept them under the table.

"You look better," Leslie said finally, breaking the silence.

Cain lifted his eyes slowly, surprised. "I feel... different," he admitted.

Leslie gave a slow nod. "Good. I'm glad."

He swallowed the lump in his throat. "I didn't expect to see you today."

"Yeah. I figured." She sipped her coffee. "I've been thinking about this moment for a long time. I rehearsed what I'd say—how I'd say it. But now that I'm sitting here with you... I don't even know where to begin."

Cain's voice cracked as he said, "You don't owe me anything, Leslie. Least of all a conversation."

"That's where you're wrong," she said softly. "I owe it to myself. To Abel. To the kids."

Cain blinked fast, trying to hold back the tears rising in his eyes.

Leslie leaned forward, placing her hands flat on the table.

"Cain, I'm not here to make you feel worse than you already do. I'm not here to punish you. Life… life already did that."

He looked down. "I still don't know what happened that day."

"I know," she said. "And I believe you. I really do."

Cain looked up at her, startled.

Leslie nodded. "You and Abel fought like brothers do. But you also loved each other deeply. He told me that. So many times. He looked up to you, Cain. Even when you didn't think he did."

A tear slipped down Cain's cheek, and he didn't bother to wipe it away.

"I've been angry. I still am, some days," she admitted. "But the anger never changed what happened. And it didn't bring Abel back. What it did do—was poison me. And I realized I couldn't raise our kids in that. I couldn't teach them bitterness and call it justice."

Cain closed his eyes, overcome by emotion.

Leslie reached across the table, resting her hand gently over his.

"I forgive you, Cain," she whispered. "Not because what happened was okay. But because holding onto that pain only deepened the hole in my heart."

Cain wept quietly, her touch grounding him.

"I'll never stop missing him," Leslie said. "But I think Abel would want me to live. I think he'd want all of us to live."

Cain nodded through the tears, unable to speak.

"The children need you too. You're their uncle," she continued. "They ask about you all the time. And I want you to be in their lives—but only if you're ready. If you're healing."

"I'm trying," he choked out. "I really am."

"I know," she said, squeezing his hand. "And that's all I needed to hear."

They sat together in silence, not as enemies but as survivors—both navigating the wreckage of a shared grief, both trying to rebuild something from the ashes.

Cain didn't know what the future would look like. But for the first time in a long while, it didn't seem so impossible. And for him, that was enough to keep going.

CHAPTER THIRTY-SIX

Sleep had long abandoned Cain. He tossed and turned, the weight of his thoughts dragging him through a restless night. He glanced over at the clock—it was 5:30 AM. Resigned, Cain threw the covers aside and gave up hope of finding rest. The house was silent as he made his way to the bathroom, the cold floor sending a shiver up his spine as he flicked on the light.

His breath caught in his throat the moment his eyes met his reflection in the mirror. He hadn't looked at himself since the night he killed his brother, and the face staring back was a stranger—hollow, broken, and heavy with guilt. Without warning, Cain collapsed to his knees, the chill of the tile seeping into his bones. Quiet sobs wracked his body as memories of Abel flooded his mind. Hours passed—or maybe it was minutes—before exhaustion finally claimed him, and he drifted into an uneasy sleep right there on the cold floor.

"Wake up, bro," a familiar voice echoed, soft but insistent. Cain's eyes fluttered open, but the sudden sight before him made him recoil in shock—his head hit the sharp corner of the sink, sending a sharp pain through his skull.

"Open your eyes, Cain," the voice urged gently.

He squeezed them shut, whispering to himself over and over, *This can't be real. This can't be real.*

"Cain, it's me," the voice said again.

His voice trembled as he whispered, "It can't be... I killed you."

"Please, open your eyes," the voice beckoned softly.

Reluctantly, Cain cracked open his eyes and found himself staring into the warm, familiar gaze of his brother. Eyes that were so much like his own, filled with a peace Cain had long forgotten.

"I don't understand," Cain whispered, shaking his head. "How? Why? This doesn't make any sense."

Abel smiled—a smile full of tenderness and love. "I miss you, Cain."

"You miss me?" Cain's voice cracked with confusion and pain. "After what I did to you?"

Abel reached out, his expression unwavering. "No matter how bad things got between us, I always knew you would never hurt me on purpose."

"Stop!" Cain's voice rose, anguish breaking through. "Stop being kind to me. I killed you. I don't deserve your kindness. I deserve to be haunted by you for the rest of my life."

Abel stood, a playful grin tugging at the corners of his mouth. "Cain, you've watched too many scary movies. Come on, let's talk."

He extended his hand. Cain hesitated, then took it, allowing his brother to help him to his feet. Together, they walked toward the bedroom.

Sitting on the edge of the bed, Cain looked at Abel with a mixture of awe and disbelief. *This has to be a dream,* he thought, *but it feels so real.*

"I miss you," Abel said quietly.

Overwhelmed, Cain collapsed to his knees again, tears flowing freely. "Please come back," he begged. "I'll trade my life for yours. I'll do anything—just come back."

Abel knelt beside him, his voice soft and steady. "It's not that simple, Cain. You have to forgive yourself."

"How?" Cain shouted, desperation in his eyes. "How do I forgive myself for killing the person I was supposed to protect?"

"That's a question only you can answer," Abel said gently. "But I can tell you this—you *must* forgive. Holding onto guilt will destroy you. It will tear apart every relationship you have with those who love you."

Abel's gaze was steady. "I see the anger inside you, Cain. Instead of lashing out, you're turning it inward and pushing away the people who care most. If you love me, forgive yourself."

"The enemy took my life," Abel said, "but don't let him take yours too."

Cain's tears slowed as he whispered, "I love you, Abel. I know I wasn't always the brother I should have been, but I love you."

Abel laughed, a warm sound that startled Cain. "Don't you think I know that? Remember when Tyrone Wilks tried to beat me up at Shaw, and you broke his jaw?"

Cain chuckled through his tears. "Yeah, he never looked your way again."

"Right," Abel said, pride lighting his eyes. "Because he knew my big brother had my back."

"What am I supposed to do without you?" Cain's voice cracked with sorrow.

"Live," Abel said quietly. "Live. I know it won't be easy, but you can forgive yourself."

Abel's voice softened. "If you love me, forgive yourself—for me. You have an amazing wife, beautiful children who adore you, parents who love you, and nieces and nephews who think you're the coolest guy alive."

"Don't cry for me, Cain. I'm in a good place. When Jesus said He'd prepare a place for us, He wasn't lying."

Abel smiled warmly. "If you want to honor me, do it by loving your wife and kids the way I know you can. Be the husband and father I always strived to be. Watch over my family, and make sure they never forget me."

Cain sobbed as he held his brother tightly. "I promise."

Slowly, his eyes fluttered open—and he was back on the cold bathroom floor. Heart pounding, Cain scrambled to his feet and rushed through the house. The vision had been so vivid, so real, he whispered to himself in disbelief.

He collapsed across his bed, clutching his pillow tightly. "Please help me, God," he sobbed. "Please help me forgive myself."

CHAPTER THIRTY-SEVEN

The morning light filtered softly through the kitchen window as Eva watched Cain leave for work, his shoulders heavy with the weight of the world. Once the door clicked shut behind him, she turned to Adam, her eyes filled with worry. "Adam, what are we going to do about Cain?" she asked, her voice trembling with the ache she felt deep inside.

Adam settled beside her at the table, his presence steady and comforting. He took her hand gently in his, his thumb tracing slow, soothing circles. "I wish I had an answer, Eva," he said quietly, stroking his distinguished gray beard thoughtfully. "As much as we want to help, this is something Cain has to work through on his own."

Eva's eyes brimmed with tears. "It's so hard watching him like this. Every night, without fail, he cries himself to sleep. Not a single night goes by without that pain consuming him."

Adam nodded solemnly, his own heart heavy. "I hear him too," he admitted softly. "The house feels so quiet, like the life's been sucked out of it since Abel's been gone."

"We have to keep praying," Adam continued, trying to hold onto hope. "Cain's doing better in some ways. He hasn't missed a single therapy session, and I've noticed something… he actually looks relieved when he comes back. Like a small weight has been lifted, even if just for a little while."

Eva smiled faintly, grateful for any sign of progress. "I've seen it too. But then, just as soon as he allows himself to feel even a hint of happiness, it's like he punishes himself. The sadness crashes back in."

Adam sighed, his voice tender but firm. "I know, baby. And as much as it hurts to watch, this is his journey. We can't fix this for him — he must find his own way through the darkness."

Eva leaned into her husband, wrapping her arms around him in a tight embrace. For a moment, they just held each other, drawing strength from their shared love and grief. The truth was undeniable—life as they had known it was forever changed. The laughter that once filled their home was gone, replaced by silence and sorrow. It felt as if a part of their souls had died along with Abel.

But Eva's heart steeled itself with quiet determination. She refused to let grief claim their joy entirely. The enemy had stolen so much already, but she would fight to protect the light that remained.

"We'll get through this," Eva whispered, her voice resolute. "Together."

CHAPTER THIRTY-EIGHT

Cain found solace in his work at the garage, partly because it kept him away from people. Having lived his entire adult life in the small city of Brandywine, Maryland, most of the community knew what he had done. He hated the way familiar faces would often look at him—some with pity, others with judgment—reminders of a past he desperately wanted to move beyond.

His boss, Glenn, was a longtime friend of his father and owned the garage where classic cars were lovingly restored. It was the perfect place for Cain. He loved working with his hands, and the smell of oil and old leather brought a comforting normalcy to his days. Glenn had known Cain since he was a baby and had been one of the first to reach out when Cain was released. Cain never forgot the kindness Glenn showed him—giving him a chance when most doors were closed.

One afternoon, as Cain sat alone in the worn lunchroom staring blankly at his sandwich, Glenn walked in. "Penny for your thoughts?" Glenn asked with a gentle smile.

Cain looked up and returned the smile. "Hey, Glenn. I was just thinking about how grateful I am that you gave me this shot. I don't know where I'd be without this job."

Glenn pulled out a chair and sat across from him at the old table. "You mind if I join you?"

"Of course not," Cain said, clearing a space.

Glenn leaned forward, his voice calm but serious. "Cain, I hired you for a few reasons. First, your parents have been dear friends for years—I'd do anything for them. Second, you're one of the best mechanics I've ever met. But lastly, and most importantly… you remind me a lot of myself."

Before Cain could respond, Glenn raised a hand to pause him.

"I served seventeen years in prison for aggravated manslaughter," Glenn confessed, eyes glistening with unshed tears. "When I was eighteen, I killed my best friend. I caught him in bed with my girlfriend. I'd never been so angry in my life. I don't even remember hitting him. When I came to, there was blood everywhere, and my girlfriend was screaming. I'd beaten him to death with something I picked up in a blind rage."

Glenn wiped his eyes, the weight of the memory pressing down on him. Cain sat stunned. Glenn was one of the kindest, calmest men he knew—he'd never imagined a story like this behind his quiet demeanor. So many questions swirled in Cain's mind, but he stayed silent, letting Glenn speak.

"I remember my parents' faces at my arraignment," Glenn continued, his voice breaking. "Never in my life had I felt such failure. I didn't care what happened to me. The despair in my mother's eyes shattered me. My father couldn't even look at me. But worst of all was the look on Tommy's mother's face… she was like a second mom to me. I was always at their house, loved him like a brother. Killing him… it broke something inside me."

Glenn paused, steadying himself. "One year, on Tommy's birthday, his mother came to visit me in prison. When I saw her face in the visitor's room, my knees buckled. The guards helped me to sit. We just sat in silence for what felt like hours but was only moments. Then she looked at me and said three simple words before walking away."

Tears spilled down Glenn's cheeks as he met Cain's eyes. "She said, 'I forgive you.'"

The raw emotion in Glenn's voice filled the room. Cain's own tears began to flow as he thought of his own parents, of his mistakes, and of the impossible burden of forgiveness.

"Cain," Glenn said softly, "forgiveness is a gift. Accept it."

Cain wept openly, finally releasing years of bottled pain as Glenn's steady hand comforted him.

Later that evening, as Cain drove home, a profound lightness settled over him. The weight that had crushed his spirit began to lift.

"Thank you, Lord," he whispered over and over, a genuine smile breaking through for the first time in a long time.

CHAPTER THIRTY-NINE

"You look different," Cam said softly as Cain stepped onto the porch, his silhouette framed by the fading light.

Cain smiled faintly and sat down beside her on the creaky swing. "I feel different," he admitted, his voice low but steady. "I had a really open, honest conversation with Glenn this morning. He gave me a new way of seeing things — something I desperately needed."

Cam nodded, her eyes warm with encouragement.

"I know this won't change everything overnight," Cain continued, "but I have to find a way to forgive myself. It's not fair for any of you to carry the weight of my mistakes."

"I'm so glad to hear that, Cain. I've been praying for you every day," Cam said, squeezing his hand gently.

"Thank you," Cain said, his smile growing a little. "I need all the prayers I can get."

Cam chuckled softly. "Don't we all?"

Suddenly, Cain glanced toward the house. "Where are the kids?"

"Inside, with your parents. They wanted to surprise you with a cake for your birthday."

Cain's chest tightened painfully. He hadn't celebrated a birthday since Abel died — in fact, he'd almost forgotten it was even coming.

Cam noticed the change in him immediately. "Are you okay?"

Cain took a few slow, steadying breaths. "Yeah, I'm fine. Just... I haven't really celebrated my birthday since..." His voice faltered.

"I'm sorry, Cain. I should have thought about that," Cam said gently. "I can talk to them if you want."

"No," Cain shook his head, a small, bittersweet smile tugging at his lips. "I can't believe they went to all this trouble for me. They really wanted to bake *me* a cake?"

"It was their idea. They begged me last night, and your mom was so excited to help," Cam explained, smiling.

Cain's smile grew more genuine. "I have a lot to make up for. I owe all of you so much."

"Cain," Cam said softly, turning to face him, "I know you never meant to hurt me or the kids. You spent so long fighting battles inside your own head. God knows I wish you could take back the pain and hurt, but we're here now."

Cain looked down, the weight of his regret heavy in his eyes.

"I'm not asking you to be perfect," Cam continued. "And I don't care how long it takes. I'm in this with you — for the long haul."

Cain's gaze lifted, searching hers. "What about the divorce papers?"

Cam laughed softly and reached into her pocket. "I tore them up." "For better or worse?" Cain asked with a hopeful grin. Cam smiled right back. "For better or worse."

Epilogue

The late afternoon sun cast a warm glow over the small backyard where laughter echoed through the air. Cain sat on the porch swing beside Cam, their fingers intertwined. Around them, the kids played with a carefree spirit Cain hadn't seen in years.

Months had passed since that pivotal morning on the porch, and life was slowly stitching itself back together. Cain's visits with Dr. Gray continued, each session peeling back layers of pain and guilt, making room for forgiveness and healing. He still wrestled with his past, but the heavy chains of shame had begun to loosen.

Adam stood nearby, watching Eva interact with their grandchildren. The smile on her face was radiant — a reflection of the hope they both fought to reclaim. Adam no longer saw the haunted man who had struggled in silence; instead, he saw a husband and father fighting to be the man they all needed.

Glenn's garage had become more than just a workplace; it was a sanctuary. Working on classic cars reminded Cain of the beauty in restoration, mirroring his own journey toward mending broken pieces of his soul.

Leslie had also been a steady presence — cautious but compassionate — gradually bridging the gaps that tragedy had torn apart. Family dinners were no longer painful reminders but moments of connection and rebuilding.

Cain looked at Cam and whispered, "Thank you… for believing in me."

Cam smiled, her eyes shimmering with tears of joy. "I always will. We're in this together — for better, for worse, and every day in between."

As the sun dipped below the horizon, Cain took a deep breath and felt, for the first time in a long while, that he was exactly where he was meant to be: surrounded by love, healing, and the promise of tomorrow.

The End

Available now on Amazon!

Job: A Modern Perspective

A contemporary retelling of the biblical story of Job—one man's unshakable faith through loss, injustice, and redemption.

Sins of a Father

A gripping generational drama about a father's return from prison, seeking redemption and a chance to rebuild his broken bond with his daughter. But can he prove he's truly changed before it's too late?

The Prodigal Sons

For Dre, his twin sister Drea, and their close group, the church was their anchor. But as life pulls them apart, faith fades—until tragedy strikes. Broken and lost, they must find their way back to the love and strength they left behind. Can faith heal what nearly tore them apart?

Coming Soon

- The Pain Behind the White Picket Fence

- Grace Under Pressure

- Love in the Balance

- Redemption Season

- A Bridge of Grace

- The Redemption of Scrooge

www.ingramcontent.com/pod-product-compliance
Lightning Source LLC
Chambersburg PA
CBHW051344020726
47501CB00007B/2253